Racketty-Packetty House

and Other Stories

FRANCES HODGSON BURNETT

DOVER PUBLICATIONS, INC.
Mineola, New York

EDITOR OF THIS VOLUME: JANET BAINE KOPITO

Published in Canada by General Publishing Company, Ltd., 895 Don Mills Road, 400-2 Park Centre, Toronto, Ontario M3C 1W3.
Published in the United Kingdom by David & Charles, Brunel House, Forde Close, Newton Abbot, Devon TQ12 4PU.

Bibliographical Note

This Dover edition, first published in 2002, is an original compilation of unabridged stories from standard editions.

Library of Congress Cataloging-in-Publication Data

Burnett, Frances Hodgson, 1849–1924.
    Racketty-packetty house and other stories / Frances Hodgson Burnett.
      p. cm. — (Dover juvenile classics)
    Original compilation of unabridged stories from standard editions.
    Summary: A collection of short stories, including "The Story of Prince Fairyfoot," "The Proud Little Grain of Wheat," and "Behind the White Brick."
    ISBN 0-486-41860-X
    1. Children's stories, American. [1. Short stories.] I. Title. II. Series.

PZ7.B934 Rae 2001
[Fic]—dc21

2001042332

Manufactured in the United States of America
Dover Publications, Inc., 31 East 2nd Street, Mineola, N.Y. 11501

Contents

	PAGE
Racketty-Packetty House	1
Sara Crewe	27
Little Saint Elizabeth	74
The Story of Prince Fairyfoot	99
The Proud Little Grain of Wheat	124
Behind the White Brick	137

Racketty-Packetty House

and Other Stories

Now this is the story about the doll family I liked and the doll family I didn't. When you read it you are to remember something I am going to tell you. This is it: If you think dolls never do anything you don't see them do, you are very much mistaken. When people are not looking at them they can do anything they choose. They can dance and sing and play on the piano and have all sorts of fun. But they can only move about and talk when people turn their backs and are not looking. If any one looks, they just stop. Fairies know this and of course Fairies visit in all the dolls' houses where the dolls are agreeable. They will not associate, though, with dolls who are not nice. They never call or leave their cards at a dolls' house where the dolls are proud or bad tempered. They are very particular. If you are conceited or ill-tempered yourself, you will never know a fairy as long as you live.

Queen Crosspatch

Racketty-Packetty House

Racketty-Packetty House was in a corner of Cynthia's nursery. And it was not in the best corner either. It was in the corner behind the door, and that was not at all a fashionable neighborhood. Racketty-Packetty House had been pushed there to be out of the way when Tidy Castle was brought in, on Cynthia's birthday. As soon as she saw Tidy Castle Cynthia did not care for Racketty-Packetty House and indeed was quite ashamed of it. She thought the corner behind the door quite good enough for such a shabby old dolls' house, when there was the beautiful new one built like a castle and furnished with the most elegant chairs and tables and carpets and curtains and ornaments and pictures and beds and baths and lamps and bookcases, and with a knocker on the front door, and a stable with a pony cart in it at the back. The minute she saw it she called out:

"Oh! What a beautiful doll castle! What shall we do with that untidy old Racketty-Packetty House now? It is too shabby and old-fashioned to stand near it."

In fact, that was the way in which the old dolls' house got its name. It had always been called, "The Dolls' House," before, but after that it was pushed into the unfashionable neighborhood behind the door and ever afterwards—when it was spoken of at all—it was just called Racketty-Packetty House, and nothing else.

Of course Tidy Castle was grand, and Tidy Castle was new and had all the modern improvements in it, and

Racketty-Packetty House was as old-fashioned as it could be. It had belonged to Cynthia's Grandmamma and had been made in the days when Queen Victoria was a little girl, and when there were no electric lights even in Princesses' dolls' houses. Cynthia's Grandmamma had kept it very neat because she had been a good house-keeper even when she was seven years old. But Cynthia was not a good housekeeper and she did not re-cover the furniture when it got dingy, or re-paper the walls, or mend the carpets and bedclothes, and she never thought of such a thing as making new clothes for the doll family, so that of course their early Victorian frocks and capes and bonnets grew in time to be too shabby for words. You see, when Queen Victoria was a little girl, dolls wore queer frocks and long pantalets and boy dolls wore funny frilled trousers and coats which it would almost make you laugh to look at.

But the Racketty-Packetty House family had known bet-ter days. I and my Fairies had known them when they were quite new and had been a birthday present just as Tidy Castle was when Cynthia turned eight years old, and there was as much fuss about them when their house arrived as Cynthia made when she saw Tidy Castle.

Cynthia's Grandmamma had danced about and clapped her hands with delight, and she had scrambled down upon her knees and taken the dolls out one by one and thought their clothes beautiful. And she had given each one of them a grand name.

"This one shall be Amelia," she said. "And this one is Charlotte, and this is Victoria Leopoldina, and this one Aurelia Matilda, and this one Leontine, and this one Clotilda, and these boys shall be Augustus and Rowland and Vincent and Charles Edward Stuart."

For a long time they led a very gay and fashionable life. They had parties and balls and were presented at Court and went to Royal Christenings and Weddings and were married themselves and had families and scarlet fever and whooping cough and funerals and every luxury. But that was long, long ago, and now all was changed. Their house had grown shabbier and shabbier, and their clothes had grown simply awful; and Aurelia Matilda and Victoria Leopoldina had been broken to bits and thrown into the dust-bin, and Leontine—who had really been the beauty of the family—had been dragged out on the hearth rug one night and had had nearly all her paint licked off and a leg chewed up by a Newfoundland puppy, so that she was a sight to behold. As for the boys, Rowland and Vincent had quite disappeared, and Charlotte and Amelia always believed they had run away to seek their fortunes, because things were in such a state at home. So the only ones who were left were Clotilda and Amelia and Charlotte and poor Leontine and Augustus and Charles Edward Stuart. Even they had their names changed.

After Leontine had had her paint licked off so that her head had white bald spots on it and she had scarcely any features, a boy cousin of Cynthia's had put a bright red spot on each cheek and painted her a turned up nose and round saucer blue eyes and a comical mouth. He and Cynthia had called her "Ridiklis" instead of Leontine, and she had been called that ever since. All the dolls were jointed Dutch dolls, so it was easy to paint any kind of features on them and stick out their arms and legs in any way you liked, and Leontine did look funny after Cynthia's cousin had finished. She certainly was not a beauty but her turned up nose and her round eyes and funny mouth always seemed to be laughing so she really was the most good-natured-looking creature you ever saw.

Charlotte and Amelia, Cynthia had called Meg and Peg, and Clotilda she called Kilmanskeg, and Augustus she called Gustibus, and Charles Edward Stuart was nothing but Peter Piper. So that was the end of their grand names.

The truth was, they went through all sorts of things, and if they had not been such a jolly lot of dolls they might have had fits and appendicitis and died of grief. But not a bit of it. If you will believe it, they got fun out of everything. They used to just scream with laughter over the new names, and they laughed so much over them that they got quite fond of them. When Meg's pink silk flounces were torn she pinned them up and didn't mind in the least, and when Peg's lace mantilla was played with by a kitten and brought back to her in rags and tags, she just put a few stitches in it and put it on again; and when Peter Piper lost almost the whole leg of one of his trousers he just laughed and said it made it easier for him to kick about and turn somersaults and he wished the other leg would tear off too.

You never saw a family have such fun. They could make up stories and pretend things and invent games out of nothing. And my Fairies were so fond of them that I couldn't keep them away from the dolls' house. They would go and have fun with Meg and Peg and Kilmanskeg and Gustibus and Peter Piper, even when I had work for them to do in Fairyland. But there, I was so fond of that shabby disrespectable family myself that I never would scold much about them, and I often went to see them. That is how I know so much about them. They were so fond of each other and so good-natured and always in such spirits that everybody who knew them was fond of them. And it was really only Cynthia who didn't know them and thought them only a lot of disreputable looking Dutch dolls—and Dutch dolls were quite out of fashion. The truth was that Cynthia was not a particularly nice little girl, and did not care much for anything unless it was quite new. But the kitten who had torn the lace mantilla got to know the family and simply loved them all, and the Newfoundland puppy was so sorry about Leontine's paint and her left leg, that he could never do enough to make up. He wanted to marry Leontine as soon as he grew old enough to wear a collar, but Leontine said she would never desert her family; because now that she wasn't the beauty any more she became the useful one, and did all the kitchen work, and sat up and made poultices and beef tea when any of the rest were ill. And the Newfoundland puppy saw she was right, for the whole family simply adored Ridiklis and could not possibly have done without her. Meg and Peg and Kilmanskeg could have married any minute if they had liked. There were two cock sparrows and a gentleman mouse, who proposed to them over and over again. They all three said they did not want fashionable wives but cheerful dispositions and a happy home. But Meg and Peg were like Ridiklis and could not bear to leave their families—besides not wanting to live in nests, and hatch eggs—and Kilmanskeg said she would die of a broken heart if she could not be with Ridiklis, and Ridiklis did not like cheese and crumbs and mousy things, so they could never live together in a mouse hole. But neither the gentleman mouse nor the sparrows were offended because the news was broken to them so sweetly and they went on visiting just as before. Everything was as shabby and disrespectable and as gay and happy as it could be until Tidy Castle was brought into the nursery and then the whole family had rather a fright.

It happened in this way:

When the dolls' house was lifted by the nurse and carried into the corner behind the door, of course it was rather an exciting and shaky thing for Meg and Peg and Kilmanskeg and Gustibus and Peter Piper (Ridiklis was out shopping). The furniture tumbled about and everybody had to hold on to anything they could catch hold of. As it was, Kilsmanskeg slid under a table and Peter Piper sat down in the coal-box; but notwithstanding all this, they did not lose their tempers and when the nurse sat their house down on the floor with a bump, they all got up and began to laugh. Then they ran and peeped out of the windows and then they ran back and laughed again.

"Well," said Peter Piper, "we have been called Meg and Peg and Kilmanskeg and Gustibus and Peter Piper instead of our grand names, and now we live in a place called Racketty-Packetty House. Who cares! Let's join hands and have a dance."

And they joined hands and danced 'round and 'round and kicked up their heels, and their rags and tatters flew about and they laughed until they fell down, one on top of the other.

It was just at this minute that Ridiklis came back. The nurse had found her under a chair and stuck her in through a window. She sat on the drawing room sofa which had holes in its covering and the stuffing coming out, and her one whole leg stuck out straight in front of her, and her bonnet and shawl were on one side and her basket was on her left arm full of things she had got cheap at market. She was out of breath and rather pale through being lifted up and swished through the air so suddenly, but her saucer eyes and her funny mouth looked as cheerful as ever.

"Good gracious, if you knew what I have just heard!" she said. They all scrambled up and called out together.

"Hello! What is it?"

"The nurse said the most awful thing," she answered them. "When Cynthia asked what she should do with this old Racketty-Packetty House, she said, 'Oh! I'll put it behind the door for the present and then it shall be carried downstairs and burned. It's too disgraceful to be kept in any decent nursery.'"

"Oh!" cried out Peter Piper.

"Oh!" said Gustibus.

"Oh! Oh! Oh!" said Meg and Peg and Kilmanskeg. "Will they burn our dear old shabby house? Do you think they will?" And actually tears began to run down their cheeks.

Peter Piper sat down on the floor all at once with his hands stuffed in his pockets.

"I don't care how shabby it is," he said. "It's a jolly nice old place and it's the only house we've ever had."

"I never want to have any other," said Meg.

Gustibus leaned against the wall with his hands stuffed in his pockets.

"I wouldn't move if I was made King of England," he said. "Buckingham Palace wouldn't be half as nice."

"We've had such fun here," said Peg. And Kilmanskeg shook her head from side to side and wiped her eyes on her ragged pocket-handkerchief. There is no knowing what would have happened to them if Peter Piper hadn't cheered up as he always did.

"I say," he said, "do you hear that noise?" They all listened and heard a rumbling. Peter Piper ran to the window and looked out and then ran back grinning.

"It's the nurse rolling up the armchair before the house to hide it, so that it won't disgrace the castle. Hooray! Hooray! If they don't see us they will forget all about us and we shall not be burned up at all. Our nice old Racketty-Packetty House will be left alone and we can enjoy ourselves more than ever—because we shan't be bothered with Cynthia—Hello! Let's all join hands and have a dance."

So they all joined hands and danced 'round in a ring again and they were so relieved that they laughed and laughed until they all tumbled down in a heap just as they had done before, and rolled about giggling and squealing. It certainly seemed as if they were quite safe for some time at least. The big easy chair hid them and both the nurse and Cynthia seemed to forget that there was such a thing as a Racketty-Packetty House in the neighborhood. Cynthia was so delighted with Tidy Castle that she played with nothing else for days and days. And instead of being jealous of their grand neighbors the Racketty-Packetty House people began to get all sorts of fun out of watching them from their own windows. Several of their windows were broken and some had rags and paper stuffed into the broken panes, but Meg and Peg and Peter Piper would go and peep out of one, and Gustibus and Kilmanskeg would peep out of another, and Ridiklis could scarcely get her dishes washed and her potatoes pared because she could see the Castle kitchen from her scullery window. It was *so* exciting!

The Castle dolls were grand beyond words, and they were all lords and ladies. These were their names. There was Lady Gwendolen Vere de Vere. She was haughty and had dark eyes and hair and carried her head thrown back and her nose in the air. There was Lady Muriel Vere de Vere, and she was cold and lovely and indifferent and looked down the bridge of her delicate nose. And there was Lady Doris, who had fluffy golden hair and laughed mockingly at everybody. And there was Lord Hubert and Lord Rupert and Lord Francis, who were all handsome enough to make you feel as if you could faint. And there was their mother, the Duchess of Tidyshire; and of course there were all sorts of maids and footmen and cooks and scullery maids and even gardeners.

"We never thought of living to see such grand society," said Peter Piper to his brothers and sisters. "It's quite a kind of blessing."

"It's almost like being grand ourselves, just to be able to watch them," said Meg and Peg and Kilmanskeg, squeezing together and flattening their noses against the attic windows.

They could see bits of the sumptuous white and gold drawing room with the Duchess sitting reading near the fire, her golden glasses upon her nose, and Lady Gwendolen playing haughtily upon the harp, and Lady Muriel coldly listening to her. Lady Doris was having her golden hair dressed by her maid in her bedroom and Lord Hubert was reading the newspaper with a high-bred air, while Lord Francis was writing letters to noblemen of his acquaintance, and Lord Rupert was—in an aristocratic manner—glancing over his love letters from ladies of title.

Kilmanskeg and Peter Piper just pinched each other with glee and squealed with delight.

"Isn't it fun," said Peter Piper. "I say; aren't they awful swells! But Lord Francis can't kick about in his trousers as I can in mine, and neither can the others. I'd like to see them try to do this"—and he turned three somersaults in the middle of the room and stood on his head on the biggest hole in the carpet—and wiggled his legs and twiggled his toes at them until they shouted so with laughing that Ridiklis ran in with a saucepan in her hand and perspiration on her forehead, because she was cooking turnips, which was all they had for dinner.

"You mustn't laugh so loud," she cried out. "If we make so much noise the Tidy Castle people will begin to complain of this being a low neighborhood and they might insist on moving away."

"Oh! Scrump!" said Peter Piper, who sometimes invented doll slang—though there wasn't really a bit of harm in him. "I wouldn't have them move away for anything. They are meat and drink to me."

"They are going to have a dinner of ten courses," sighed Ridiklis. "I can see them cooking it from my scullery window. And I have nothing but turnips to give you."

"Who cares!" said Peter Piper. "Let's have ten courses of turnips and pretend each course is exactly like the one they are having at the Castle."

"I like turnips almost better than anything—almost—perhaps not quite," said Gustibus. "I can eat ten courses of turnips like a shot."

"Let's go and find out what their courses are," said Meg and Peg and Kilmanskeg, "and then we will write a menu on a piece of pink tissue paper."

And if you'll believe it, that was what they did. They divided their turnips into ten courses and they called the first one "Hors d'œuvres," and the last one "Ices," with a French name, and Peter Piper kept jumping up from the table and pretending he was a footman and flourishing about in his flapping rags of trousers and announcing the names of the dishes in such a grand way that they laughed till they nearly died, and said they never had had such a splendid dinner in their lives, and that they would rather live behind the door and watch the Tidy Castle people than be the Tidy Castle people themselves.

And then of course they all joined hands and danced 'round and 'round and kicked up their heels for joy, because they always did that whenever there was the least excuse for it—and quite often when there wasn't any at all, just because it was such good exercise and worked off their high spirits so that they could settle down for a while.

This was the way things went on day after day. They almost lived at their windows. They watched the Tidy Castle family get up and be dressed by their maids and valets in different clothes almost every day. They saw them drive out in their carriages, and have parties, and go to balls. They all nearly had brain fever with delight the day they watched Lady Gwendolen and Lady Muriel and Lady Doris, dressed in their Court trains and feathers, going to be presented at the first Drawing Room.

After the lovely creatures had gone the whole family sat down in a circle 'round the Racketty-Packetty House library fire, and Ridiklis read aloud to them about Drawing Rooms, out of a scrap of the Lady's Pictorial she had found, and after that they had a Court Drawing Room of their own, and they made tissue paper trains and glass bead crowns for diamond tiaras, and sometimes Gustibus pretended to be the Royal family, and the others were presented to him and kissed his hand, and then the others took turns and he was presented. And suddenly the most delightful thing occurred to Peter Piper. He thought it would be rather nice to make them all into lords and ladies and he did it by touching them on the shoulder with the drawing room poker which he straightened because it was so crooked that it was almost bent double. It is not exactly the way such things are done at Court, but Peter Piper thought it would do—and at any rate it was great fun. So he made them all kneel down in a row and he touched each on the shoulder with the poker and said:

"Rise up, Lady Meg and Lady Peg and Lady Kilmanskeg and Lady Ridiklis of Racketty-Packetty House—and also the Right Honorable Lord Gustibus Rags!" And they all jumped up at once and made bows and curtsied to each other. But they made Peter Piper into a Duke, and he was called the Duke of Tags. He knelt down on the big hole in the carpet and each one of them gave him a little thump on the shoulder with the poker, because it took more thumps to make a Duke than a common or garden Lord.

The day after this another much more exciting thing took place. The nurse was in a bad temper and when she was tidying the nursery she pushed the easy chair aside and saw Racketty-Packetty House.

"Oh!" she said. "There is that Racketty-Packetty old thing still. I had forgotten it. It must be carried downstairs and burned. I will go and tell one of the footmen to come for it."

Meg and Peg and Kilmanskeg were in their attic and they all rushed out in such a hurry to get downstairs that they rolled all the way down the staircase, and Peter Piper and Gustibus had to dart out of the drawing room and pick them up. Ridiklis came staggering up from the kitchen quite out of breath.

"Oh! Our house is going to be burned! Our house is going to be burned!" cried Meg and Peg clutching their brothers.

"Let us go and throw ourselves out of the window!" cried Kilmanskeg.

"I don't see how they can have the heart to burn a person's home!" said Ridiklis, wiping her eyes with her kitchen duster.

Peter Piper was rather pale, but he was extremely brave and remembered that he was the head of the family.

"Now, Lady Meg and Lady Peg and Lady Kilmanskeg," he said, "let us all keep cool."

"We shan't keep cool when they set our house on fire," said Gustibus. Peter Piper just snapped his fingers.

"Pooh!" he said. "We are only made of wood and it won't hurt a bit. We shall just snap and crackle and go off almost like fireworks and then we shall be ashes and fly away into the air and see all sorts of things. Perhaps it may be more fun than anything we have done yet."

"But our nice old house! Our nice old Racketty-Packetty House," said Ridiklis. "I do so love it. The kitchen is so convenient—even though the oven won't bake any more."

And things looked most serious because the nurse really was beginning to push the armchair away. But it would not move and I will tell you why. One of my Fairies, who had come down the chimney when they were talking, had called me and I had come in a second with a whole army of my Workers, and though the nurse couldn't see them, they were all holding the chair tight down on the carpet so that it would not stir.

And I—Queen Crosspatch—myself—flew downstairs and made the footman remember that minute that a box had come for Cynthia and that he must take it upstairs to her nursery. If I had not been on the spot he would have forgotten it until it was too late. But just in the very nick of time up he came, and Cynthia sprang up as soon as she saw him.

"Oh!" she cried out. "It must be the doll who broke her little leg and was sent to the hospital. It must be Lady Patsy."

And she opened the box and gave a little scream of joy for there lay Lady Patsy (her whole name was Patricia) in a lace-frilled nightgown, with her lovely leg in bandages and a pair of tiny crutches and a trained nurse by her side.

That was how I saved them that time. There was such excitement over Lady Patsy and her little crutches and her nurse that nothing else was thought of and my Fairies pushed the armchair back and Racketty-Packetty House was hidden and forgotten once more.

The whole Racketty-Packetty family gave a great gasp of joy and sat down in a ring all at once, on the floor, mopping their foreheads with anything they could get hold of. Peter Piper used an antimacassar.

"Oh! We are obliged to you, Queen B-bell—Patch," he panted out, "but these alarms of fire are upsetting."

"You leave them to me," I said, "and I'll attend to them. Tip!" I commanded the Fairy nearest me. "You will have to stay about here and be ready to give the alarm when anything threatens to happen." And I flew away, feeling I had done a good morning's work. Well, that was the beginning of a great many things, and many of them were connected with Lady Patsy; and but for me there might have been unpleasantness.

Of course the Racketty-Packetty dolls forgot about their fright directly, and began to enjoy themselves again as usual. That was their way. They never sat up all night with Trouble, Peter Piper used to say. And I told him they were quite right. If you make a fuss over trouble and put it to bed and nurse it and give it beef tea and gruel, you can never get rid of it.

Their great delight now was Lady Patsy. They thought she was prettier than any of the other Tidy Castle dolls. She neither turned her nose up, nor looked down the bridge of it, nor laughed mockingly. She had dimples in the corners of her mouth and long curly lashes and her nose was saucy and her eyes were bright and full of laughs.

"She's the clever one of the family," said Peter Piper. "I am sure of that."

She was treated as an invalid at first, of course, and kept in her room; but they could see her sitting up in her frilled nightgown. After a few days she was carried to a soft chair by the window and there she used to sit and look out; and the Racketty-Packetty House dolls crowded 'round their window and adored her.

After a few days, they noticed that Peter Piper was often missing and one morning Ridiklis went up into the attic and found him sitting at a window all by himself and staring and staring.

"Oh! Duke," she said (you see they always tried to remember each other's titles). "Dear me, Duke, what are you doing here?"

"I am looking at her," he answered. "I'm in love. I fell in love with her the minute Cynthia took her out of her box. I am going to marry her."

"But she's a lady of high degree," said Ridiklis quite alarmed.

"That's why she'll have me," said Peter Piper in his

most cheerful manner. "Ladies of high degree always marry the good-looking ones in rags and tatters. If I had a whole suit of clothes on, she wouldn't look at me. I'm very good-looking, you know," and he turned round and winked at Ridiklis in such a delightful saucy way that she suddenly felt as if he *was* very good-looking, though she had not thought of it before.

"Hello," he said all at once. "I've just thought of something to attract her attention. Where's the ball of string?"

Cynthia's kitten had made them a present of a ball of string which had been most useful. Ridiklis ran and got it, and all the others came running upstairs to see what Peter Piper was going to do. They all were delighted to hear he had fallen in love with the lovely, funny Lady Patsy. They found him standing in the middle of the attic unrolling the ball of string.

"What are you going to do, Duke?" they all shouted.

"Just you watch," he said, and he began to make the string into a rope ladder—as fast as lightning. When he had finished it, he fastened one end of it to a beam and swung the other end out of the window.

"From her window," he said, "she can see Racketty-Packetty House and I'll tell you something. She's always looking at it. She watches us as much as we watch her, and I have seen her giggling and giggling when we were having fun. Yesterday when I chased Lady Meg and Lady Peg and Lady Kilmanskeg 'round and 'round the front of the house and turned somersaults every five steps, she laughed until she had to stuff her handkerchief into her mouth. When we joined hands and danced and laughed until we fell in heaps I thought she was going to have a kind of rosy-dimpled, lovely little fit, she giggled so. If I run down the side of the house on this rope ladder it will attract her attention and then I shall begin to do things."

He ran down the ladder and that very minute they saw Lady Patsy at her window give a start and lean forward to look. They all crowded 'round their window and chuckled and chuckled as they watched him.

He turned three stately somersaults and stood on his feet and made a cheerful bow. The Racketty-Packettys saw Lady Patsy begin to giggle that minute. Then he took an antimacassar out of his pocket and fastened it 'round the edge of his torn trousers leg, as if it were lace trimming and began to walk about like a Duke—with his arms folded on his chest and his ragged old hat cocked on one side over his ear. Then the Racketty-Packettys saw Lady Patsy begin to laugh. Then Peter Piper stood on his head and kissed his hand and Lady Patsy covered her face and rocked backwards and forwards in her chair laughing and laughing.

Then he struck an attitude with his tattered leg put forward gracefully and he pretended he had a guitar and he sang—right up at her window.

> *"From Racketty-Packetty House I come,*
> *It stands, dear Lady, in a slum,*
> *A low, low slum behind the door*
> *The stout armchair is placed before,*
> *(Just take a look at it, my Lady).*

> *"The house itself is a perfect sight,*
> *And everybody's dressed like a perfect fright,*
> *But no one cares a single jot*
> *And each one giggles over his lot,*
> *(And as for me, I'm in love with you).*

> *"I can't make up another verse,*
> *And if I did it would be worse,*
> *But I could stand and sing all day,*
> *If I could think of things to say,*
> *(But the fact is I just wanted to make*
> *   you look at me)."*

And then he danced such a lively jig that his rags and tags flew about him, and then he made another bow and kissed his hand again and ran up the ladder like a flash and jumped into the attic.

After that Lady Patsy sat at her window all the time and would not let the trained nurse put her to bed at all; and Lady Gwendolen and Lady Muriel and Lady Doris could not understand it. Once Lady Gwendolen said haughtily and disdainfully and scornfully and scathingly:

"If you sit there so much, those low Racketty-Packetty House people will think you are looking at them."

"I am," said Lady Patsy, showing all her dimples at once. "They are such fun."

And Lady Gwendolen swooned haughtily away, and the trained nurse could scarcely restore her.

When the castle dolls drove out or walked in their garden, the instant they caught sight of one of the Racketty-Packettys they turned up their noses and sniffed aloud, and several times the Duchess said she would remove because the neighborhood was absolutely low. They all scorned the Racketty-Packetty's—they just *scorned* them.

One moonlight night Lady Patsy was sitting at her window and she heard a whistle in the garden. When she peeped out carefully, there stood Peter Piper waving his ragged cap at her, and he had his rope ladder under his arm.

"Hello," he whispered as loud as he could. "Could you catch a bit of rope if I threw it up to you?"

"Yes," she whispered back.

"Then catch this," he whispered again and threw up the end of a string and she caught it the first throw. It was fastened to the rope ladder.

"Now pull," he said.

She pulled and pulled until the rope ladder reached her window and then she fastened that to a hook under the sill and the first thing that happened—just like lightning— was that Peter Piper ran up the ladder and leaned over her window ledge.

"Will you marry me," he said. "I haven't anything to give you to eat and I am as ragged as a scarecrow, but will you?"

She clapped her hands.

"I eat very little," she said. "And I would do without anything at all, if I could live in your funny old shabby house."

"It is a ridiculous, tumbled-down old barn, isn't it?" he said. "But every one of us is as nice as we can be. We are perfect Turkish Delights. It's laughing that does it. Would you like to come down the ladder and see what a jolly, shabby old hole the place is?"

"Oh! Do take me," said Lady Patsy.

So he helped her down the ladder and took her under the armchair and into Racketty-Packetty House and Meg and Peg and Kilmanskeg and Ridiklis and Gustibus all crowded 'round her and gave little screams of joy at the sight of her.

They were afraid to kiss her at first, even though she was engaged to Peter Piper. She was so pretty and her frock had so much lace on it that they were afraid their old rags might spoil her. But she did not care about her lace and flew at them and kissed and hugged them every one.

"I have so wanted to come here," she said. "It's so dull at the Castle I had to break my leg just to get a change. The Duchess sits reading near the fire with her gold eyeglasses on her nose and Lady Gwendolen plays haughtily on the harp and Lady Muriel coldly listens to her, and Lady Doris is always laughing mockingly, and Lord Hubert reads the newspaper with a high-bred air, and Lord Francis writes letters to noblemen of his acquaintance, and Lord Rupert glances over his love letters from ladies of title, in an aristocratic manner—until I could *scream*. Just to see you dears dancing about in your rags and tags and laughing and inventing games as if you didn't mind anything, is such a relief."

She nearly laughed her little curly head off when they all went 'round the house with her, and Peter Piper showed her the holes in the carpet and the stuffing coming out of the sofas, and the feathers out of the beds, and the legs tumbling off the chairs. She had never seen anything like it before.

"At the Castle, nothing is funny at all," she said. "And nothing ever sticks out or hangs down or tumbles off. It is so plain and new."

"But I think we ought to tell her, Duke," Ridiklis said. "We may have our house burned over our heads any day." She really stopped laughing for a whole minute when she heard that, but she was rather like Peter Piper in disposition and she said almost immediately:

"Oh! They'll never do it. They've forgotten you." And Peter Piper said:

"Don't let's think of it. Let's all join hands and dance 'round and 'round and kick up our heels and laugh as hard as ever we can."

And they did—and Lady Patsy laughed harder than any one else. After that she was always stealing away from Tidy Castle and coming in and having fun. Sometimes she stayed all night and slept with Meg and Peg and everybody invented new games and stories and they really never went to bed until daylight. But the Castle dolls grew more and more scornful every day, and tossed their heads higher and higher and sniffed louder and louder until it sounded as if they all had influenza. They never lost an opportunity of saying disdainful things and once the Duchess wrote a letter to Cynthia, saying that she insisted on removing to a decent neighborhood. She laid the letter in her desk but the gentleman mouse came in the night and carried it away. So Cynthia never saw it and I don't believe she could have read it if she had seen it because the Duchess wrote very badly—even for a doll.

And then what do you suppose happened? One morning Cynthia began to play that all the Tidy Castle dolls had scarlet fever. She said it had broken out in the night and she undressed them all and put them into bed and gave them medicine. She could not find Lady Patsy, so *she* escaped the contagion. The truth was that Lady Patsy had stayed all night at Racketty-Packetty House, where they were giving an imitation Court Ball with Peter Piper in a tin crown, and shavings for supper—because they had nothing else, and in fact the gentleman mouse had brought the shavings from his nest as a present.

Cynthia played nearly all day and the Duchess and Lady Gwendolen and Lady Muriel and Lady Doris and Lord Hubert and Lord Francis and Lord Rupert got worse and worse.

By evening they were all raging in delirium and Lord Francis and Lady Gwendolen had strong mustard plasters on their chests. And right in the middle of their agony Cynthia suddenly got up and went away and left them to their fate—just as if it didn't matter in the least. Well in the middle of the night Meg and Peg and Lady Patsy wakened all at once.

"Do you hear a noise?" said Meg, lifting her head from her ragged old pillow.

"Yes, I do," said Peg, sitting up and holding her ragged old blanket up to her chin.

Lady Patsy jumped up with feathers sticking up all over her hair, because they had come out of the holes in the ragged old bed. She ran to the window and listened.

"Oh! Meg and Peg!" she cried out. "It comes from the Castle. Cynthia has left them all raving in delirium and they are all shouting and groaning and screaming."

Meg and Peg jumped up too.

"Let's go and call Kilmanskeg and Ridiklis and Gustibus and Peter Piper," they said, and they rushed to the staircase and met Kilmanskeg and Ridiklis and Gustibus and Peter Piper coming scrambling up panting because the noise had wakened them as well.

They were all over at Tidy Castle in a minute. They just tumbled over each other to get there—the kind-hearted things. The servants were every one fast asleep, though the noise was awful. The loudest groans came from Lady Gwendolen and Lord Francis because their mustard plasters were blistering them frightfully.

Ridiklis took charge, because she was the one who knew the most about illness. She sent Gustibus to waken the servants and then ordered hot water and cold water, and ice, and brandy, and poultices, and shook the trained nurse for not attending to her business—and took off the mustard plasters and gave gruel and broth and cough syrup and castor oil and ipecacuanha, and every one of the Racketty-Packettys massaged, and soothed, and patted, and put wet cloths on heads, until the fever was gone and the Castle dolls all lay back on their pillows pale and weak, but smiling faintly at every Racketty-Packetty they saw, instead of turning up their noses and tossing their heads and sniffing loudly, and just *scorning* them.

Lady Gwendolen spoke first and instead of being haughty and disdainful, she was as humble as a newborn kitten.

"Oh! You dear, shabby, disrespectable darling things!" she said. "Never, never, will I scorn you again. Never, never!"

"That's right!" said Peter Piper in his cheerful, rather slangy way. "You take my tip—never you scorn any one again. It's a mistake. Just you watch me stand on my head. It'll cheer you up."

And he turned six somersaults—just like lightning—and stood on his head and wiggled his ragged legs at them until suddenly they heard a snort from one of the beds and it was Lord Hubert beginning to laugh and then Lord Francis laughed and then Lord Hubert shouted, and then Lady Doris squealed, and Lady Muriel screamed, and Lady Gwendolen and the Duchess rolled over and over in their beds, laughing as if they would have fits.

"Oh! You delightful, funny, shabby old loves!" Lady Gwendolen kept saying. "To think that we scorned you."

"They'll be all right after this," said Peter Piper. "There's nothing cures scarlet fever like cheering up. Let's all join hands and dance 'round and 'round once for them before we go back to bed. It'll throw them into a nice light perspiration and they'll drop off and sleep like tops." And they did it, and before they had finished, the whole lot of them were perspiring gently and snoring as softly as lambs.

When they went back to Racketty-Packetty House they talked a good deal about Cynthia and wondered and wondered why she had left her scarlet fever so suddenly. And at last Ridiklis made up her mind to tell them something she had heard.

"The Duchess told me," she said, rather slowly because it was bad news—"The Duchess said that Cynthia went away because her Mama had sent for her—and her Mama had sent for her to tell her that a little girl princess is coming to see her tomorrow. Cynthia's Mama used to be a maid of honor to the Queen and that's why the little girl Princess is coming. The Duchess said—" and here Ridiklis spoke very slowly indeed, "that the nurse was so excited she said she did not know whether she stood on her head or her heels, and she must tidy up the nursery and have that Racketty-Packetty old dolls' house carried downstairs and burned, early tomorrow morning. That's what the Duchess *said*—"

Meg and Peg and Kilmanskeg clutched at their hearts and gasped and Gustibus groaned and Lady Patsy caught Peter Piper by the arm to keep from falling. Peter Piper gulped—and then he had a sudden cheerful thought.

"Perhaps she was raving in delirium," he said.

"No, she wasn't," said Ridiklis shaking her head. "I had just given her hot water and cold, and gruel, and broth, and castor oil, and ipecacuanha and put ice almost all over her. She was as sensible as any of us. Tomorrow morning we shall not have a house over our heads," and she put her ragged old apron over her face and cried.

"If she wasn't raving in delirium," said Peter Piper, "we shall not have any heads. You had better go back to the Castle tonight, Patsy. Racketty-Packetty House is no place for you."

Then Lady Patsy drew herself up so straight that she nearly fell over backwards.

"I—will—*never*—leave you!" she said, and Peter Piper couldn't make her.

You can just imagine what a doleful night it was. They

went all over the house together and looked at every hole in the carpet and every piece of stuffing sticking out of the dear old shabby sofas, and every broken window and chairleg and table and ragged blanket—and the tears ran down their faces for the first time in their lives. About six o'clock in the morning Peter Piper made a last effort.

"Let's all join hands in a circle," he said quite faintly, "and dance 'round and 'round once more."

But it was no use. When they joined hands they could not dance, and when they found they could not dance they all tumbled down in a heap and cried instead of laughing and Lady Patsy lay with her arms 'round Peter Piper's neck.

Now here is where I come in again—Queen Crosspatch— who is telling you this story. I always come in just at the nick of time when people like the Racketty-Packettys are in trouble. I walked in at seven o'clock.

"Get up off the floor," I said to them all and they got up and stared at me. They actually thought I did not know what had happened.

"A little girl Princess is coming this morning," said Peter Piper, "and our house is going to be burned over our heads. This is the end of Racketty-Packetty House."

"No, it isn't!" I said. "You leave this to me. I told the Princess to come here, though she doesn't know it in the least."

A whole army of my Working Fairies began to swarm in at the nursery window. The nurse was working very hard to put things in order and she had not sense enough to see Fairies at all. So she did not see mine, though there were hundreds of them. As soon as she made one corner tidy, they ran after her and made it untidy. They held her back by her dress and hung and swung on her apron until she could scarcely move and kept wondering why she was so slow. She could not make the nursery tidy and she was so flurried she forgot all about Racketty-Packetty House again—especially as my Working Fairies pushed the armchair close up to it so that it was quite hidden. And there it was when the little girl Princess came with her Ladies in Waiting. My Fairies had only just allowed the nurse to finish the nursery.

Meg and Peg and Kilmanskeg and Ridiklis and Gustibus and Peter Piper and Lady Patsy were huddled up together looking out of one window. They could not bear to be parted. I sat on the arm of the big chair and ordered my Working Fairies to stand ready to obey me the instant I spoke.

The Princess was a nice child and was very polite to Cynthia when she showed her all her dolls, and last but not least, Tidy Castle itself. She looked at all the rooms and the furniture and said polite and admiring things about each of them. But Cynthia realized that she was not so much interested in it as she had thought she would be. The fact was that the Princess had so many grand dolls' houses in her palace that Tidy Castle did not surprise her at all. It was just when Cynthia was finding this out that I gave the order to my Working Fairies.

"Push the armchair away," I commanded, "very slowly, so that no one will know it is being moved."

So they moved it away—very, very slowly—and no one saw that it had stirred. But the next minute the little girl Princess gave a delightful start.

"Oh! What is that!" she cried out, hurrying towards the unfashionable neighborhood behind the door.

Cynthia blushed all over and the nurse actually turned pale. The Racketty-Packettys tumbled down in a heap beneath their window and began to say their prayers very fast.

"It is only a shabby old dolls' house, your Highness," Cynthia stammered out. "It belonged to my Grandmamma, and it ought not to be in the nursery. I thought you had had it burned, Nurse!"

"Burned!" the little girl Princess cried out in the most shocked way. "Why if it was mine, I wouldn't have it burned for worlds! Oh! Please push the chair away and let me look at it. There are no dolls' houses like it anywhere in these days." And when the armchair was pushed aside she scrambled down on to her knees just as if she was not a little girl Princess at all.

"Oh! Oh! Oh!" she said. "How funny and dear! What a darling old dolls' house. It is shabby and wants mending, of course, but it is almost exactly like one my Grand-mamma had—she kept it among her treasures and only let me look at it as a great, great treat."

Cynthia gave a gasp, for the little girl Princess's Grand-mamma had been the Queen and people had knelt down and kissed her hand and had been obliged to go out of the room backwards before her.

The little girl Princess was simply filled with joy. She picked up Meg and Peg and Kilmanskeg and Gustibus and Peter Piper as if they had been really a Queen's dolls.

"Oh! The darling dears," she said. "Look at their nice, queer faces and their funny clothes. Just—just like Grand-mamma's dollies' clothes. Only these poor things do so want new ones. Oh! How I should like to dress them again just as they used to be dressed, and have the house all made just as it used to be when it was new."

"That old Racketty-Packetty House," said Cynthia, los-ing her breath.

"If it were mine I should make it just like Grandmamma's and I should love it more than any dolls' house I have. I never—never—never saw anything as nice and laughing and good-natured as these dolls' faces. They look as if they had been having fun ever since they were born. Oh! If you were to burn them and their home I—I could never forgive you!"

"I never—never—will, your Highness," stammered Cyn-thia, quite overwhelmed. Suddenly she started forward.

"Why, there is the lost doll!" she cried out. "There is Lady Patsy. How did she get into Racketty-Packetty House?"

"Perhaps she went there to see them because they were so poor and shabby," said the little girl Princess. "Perhaps she likes this one," and she pointed to Peter Piper. "Do you know when I picked him up their arms were about each other. Please let her stay with him. Oh!" she cried out the next instant and jumped a little. "I felt as if the boy one kicked his leg."

And it was actually true, because Peter Piper could not help it and he had kicked out his ragged leg for joy. He had to be very careful not to kick any more when he heard what happened next.

As the Princess liked Racketty-Packetty House so much, Cynthia gave it to her for a present—and the Princess was really happy—and before she went away she made a little speech to the whole Racketty-Packetty family, whom she had set all in a row in the ragged old, dear old, shabby old drawing room where they had had so much fun.

"You are going to come and live with me, funny, good-natured loves," she said. "And you shall all be dressed beautifully again and your house shall be mended and papered and painted and made as lovely as ever it was. And I am going to like you better than all my other dolls' houses—just as Grandmamma said she liked hers." And then she was gone.

And every bit of it came true. Racketty-Packetty House was carried to a splendid Nursery in a Palace, and Meg and Peg and Kilmanskeg and Ridiklis and Gustibus and Peter Piper were made so gorgeous that if they had not been so nice they would have grown proud. But they didn't. They only grew jollier and jollier and Peter Piper married Lady Patsy, and Ridiklis's left leg was mended and she was painted into a beauty again—but she always remained the useful one. And the dolls in the other dolls' houses used to make deep curtsies when a Racketty-Pack-etty House doll passed them, and Peter Piper could scarcely stand it because it always made him want to stand on his head and laugh—and so when they were curtsied at—because they were related to the Royal Dolls' House—they used to run into their drawing room and fall into fits of giggles and they could only stop them by all joining hands together in a ring and dancing 'round and 'round and 'round and kicking up their heels and laughing until they tumbled down in a heap.

And what do you think of that for a story. And doesn't it prove to you what a valuable Friend a Fairy is—particularly a Queen one?

Sara Crewe
or
What Happened at Miss Minchin's

In the first place, Miss Minchin lived in London. Her home was a large, dull, tall one, in a large, dull square, where all the houses were alike, and all the sparrows were alike, and where all the door-knockers made the same heavy sound, and on still days—and nearly all the days were still—seemed to resound through the entire row in which the knock was knocked. On Miss Minchin's door there was a brass plate. On the brass plate there was inscribed in black letters,

MISS MINCHIN'S

SELECT SEMINARY FOR YOUNG LADIES

Little Sara Crewe never went in or out of the house without reading that door-plate and reflecting upon it. By the time she was twelve, she had decided that all her trouble arose because, in the first place, she was not "Select," and in the second, she was not a "Young Lady." When she was eight years old, she had been brought to Miss Minchin as a pupil, and left with her. Her papa had brought her all the way from India. Her mamma had died when she was a baby, and her papa had kept her with him as long as he could. And then, finding the hot climate was making her very delicate, he had brought her to England and left her with Miss Minchin, to be part of the Select Seminary for Young Ladies. Sara, who had always been a sharp little child, who remembered things, recollected hearing him say that he had not a relative in the world whom he knew of, and so he was obliged to place her at a boarding-school, and he had heard Miss Minchin's establishment spoken of very highly. The same day, he took Sara out and bought her a great many beautiful clothes—clothes so grand and rich that only a very young and inexperienced man would have bought them for a mite of a child who was to be brought up in a boarding-school. But the fact was that he was a rash, innocent young man, and very sad at the thought of parting with his little girl, who was all he had left to remind him of her beautiful mother, whom he had dearly loved. And he wished her to have everything the most fortunate little girl could have; and so, when the polite saleswomen in the shops said, "Here is our very latest thing in hats, the plumes are exactly the same as those we sold to Lady Diana Sinclair yesterday," he immediately bought what was offered to him, and paid whatever was asked. The consequence was that Sara had a most extraordinary wardrobe. Her dresses were silk and velvet and India cashmere, her hats and bonnets were covered with bows and plumes, her small undergarments were adorned with real lace, and she returned in the cab to Miss Minchin's with a doll almost as large as herself, dressed quite as grandly as herself, too.

Then her papa gave Miss Minchin some money and went away, and for several days Sara would neither touch the doll, nor her breakfast, nor her dinner, nor her tea, and would do nothing but crouch in a small corner by the window and cry. She cried so much, indeed, that she made herself ill. She was a queer little child, with old-fashioned ways and strong feelings, and she had adored her papa, and could not be made to think that India and an interesting bungalow were not better for her than London and Miss Minchin's Select Seminary. The instant she had entered the house, she had begun promptly to hate Miss Minchin, and to think little of Miss Amelia Minchin, who was smooth and dumpy, and lisped, and was evidently afraid of her older sister. Miss Minchin was tall, and had large, cold, fishy eyes, and large, cold hands, which seemed fishy, too, because they were damp and made chills run down Sara's back when they touched her, as Miss Minchin pushed her hair off her forehead and said:

"A most beautiful and promising little girl, Captain Crewe. She will be a favorite pupil; *quite* a favorite pupil, I see."

For the first year she was a favorite pupil; at least she was indulged a great deal more than was good for her. And when the Select Seminary went walking, two by two, she was always decked out in her grandest clothes, and led by the hand, at the head of the genteel procession, by Miss Minchin herself. And when the parents of any of the pupils came, she was always dressed and called into the parlor with her doll; and she used to hear Miss Minchin say that her father was a distinguished Indian officer, and she would be heiress to a great fortune. That her father had inherited a great deal of money, Sara had heard before; and also that some day it would be hers, and that he would not remain long in the army, but would come to live in London. And every time a letter came, she hoped it would say he was coming, and they were to live together again.

But about the middle of the third year a letter came bringing very different news. Because he was not a business man himself, her papa had given his affairs into the hands of a friend he trusted. The friend had deceived and robbed him. All the money was gone, no one knew exactly where, and the shock was so great to the poor, rash young officer, that, being attacked by jungle fever shortly afterward, he had no strength to rally, and so died, leaving Sara, with no one to take care of her.

Miss Minchin's cold and fishy eyes had never looked so

cold and fishy as they did when Sara went into the parlor, on being sent for, a few days after the letter was received.

No one had said anything to the child about mourning, so, in her old-fashioned way, she had decided to find a black dress for herself, and had picked out a black velvet she had outgrown, and came into the room in it, looking the queerest little figure in the world, and a sad little figure too. The dress was too short and too tight, her face was white, her eyes had dark rings around them, and her doll, wrapped in a piece of old black crape, was held under her arm. She was not a pretty child. She was thin, and had a weird, interesting little face, short black hair, and very large, green-gray eyes fringed all around with heavy black lashes.

"I am the ugliest child in the school," she had said once, after staring at herself in the glass for some minutes.

But there had been a clever, good-natured little French teacher who had said to the music-master:

"Zat leetle Crewe. Vat a child! A so ogly beauty! Ze so large eyes! ze so little spirituelle face. Waid till she grow up. You shall see!"

This morning, however, in the tight, small black frock, she looked thinner and odder than ever, and her eyes were fixed on Miss Minchin with a queer steadiness as she slowly advanced into the parlor, clutching her doll.

"Put your doll down!" said Miss Minchin.

"No," said the child, "I won't put her down; I want her with me. She is all I have. She has stayed with me all the time since my papa died."

She had never been an obedient child. She had had her own way ever since she was born, and there was about her an air of silent determination under which Miss Minchin had always felt secretly uncomfortable. And that lady felt even now that perhaps it would be as well not to insist on her point. So she looked at her as severely as possible.

"You will have no time for dolls in future," she said; "you will have to work and improve yourself, and make yourself useful."

Sara kept the big odd eyes fixed on her teacher and said nothing.

"Everything will be very different now," Miss Minchin went on. "I sent for you to talk to you and make you understand. Your father is dead. You have no friends. You have no money. You have no home and no one to take care of you."

The little pale olive face twitched nervously, but the green-gray eyes did not move from Miss Minchin's, and still Sara said nothing.

"What are you staring at?" demanded Miss Minchin sharply. "Are you so stupid you don't understand what I mean? I tell you that you are quite alone in the world, and have no one to do anything for you, unless I choose to keep you here."

The truth was, Miss Minchin was in her worst mood. To be suddenly deprived of a large sum of money yearly and a show pupil, and to find herself with a little beggar on her hands, was more than she could bear with any degree of calmness.

"Now listen to me," she went on, "and remember what I say. If you work hard and prepare to make yourself useful in a few years, I shall let you stay here. You are only a child, but you are a sharp child, and you pick up things almost without being taught. You speak French very well, and in a year or so you can begin to help with the younger pupils. By the time you are fifteen you ought to be able to do that much at least."

"I can speak French better than you, now," said Sara; "I always spoke it with my papa in India." Which was not at all polite, but was painfully true; because Miss Minchin could not speak French at all, and, indeed, was not in the least a clever person. But she was a hard, grasping business woman; and, after the first shock of disappointment, had seen that at very little expense to herself she might prepare this clever, determined child to be very useful to her and save her the necessity of paying large salaries to teachers of languages.

"Don't be impudent, or you will be punished," she said. "You will have to improve your manners if you expect to earn your bread. You are not a parlor boarder now. Remember that if you don't please me, and I send you away, you have no home but the street. You can go now."

Sara turned away.

"Stay," commanded Miss Minchin, "don't you intend to thank me?"

Sara turned toward her. The nervous twitch was to be seen again in her face, and she seemed to be trying to control it.

"What for?" she said.

"For my kindness to you," replied Miss Minchin. "For my kindness in giving you a home."

Sara went two or three steps nearer to her. Her thin little chest was heaving up and down, and she spoke in a strange, unchildish voice.

"You are not kind," she said. "You are not kind." And she turned again and went out of the room, leaving Miss Minchin staring after her strange, small figure in stony anger.

The child walked up the staircase, holding tightly to her doll; she meant to go to her bedroom, but at the door she was met by Miss Amelia.

"You are not to go in there," she said. "That is not your room now."

"Where is my room?" asked Sara.

"You are to sleep in the attic next to the cook."

Sara walked on. She mounted two flights more, and reached the door of the attic room, opened it and went in, shutting it behind her. She stood against it and looked about her. The room was slanting-roofed and whitewashed; there was a rusty grate, an iron bedstead, and some odd articles of furniture, sent up from better rooms below, where they had been used until they were considered to be worn out. Under the skylight in the roof, which showed nothing but an oblong piece of dull gray sky, there was a battered old red footstool.

Sara went to it and sat down. She was a queer child, as I have said before, and quite unlike other children. She seldom cried. She did not cry now. She laid her doll, Emily, across her knees, and put her face down upon her, and her arms around her, and sat there, her little black head resting on the black crape, not saying one word, not making one sound.

From that day her life changed entirely. Sometimes she used to feel as if it must be another life altogether, the life of some other child. She was a little drudge and outcast; she was given her lessons at odd times and expected to learn without being taught; she was sent on errands by Miss Minchin, Miss Amelia and the cook. Nobody took any notice of her except when they ordered her about. She was often kept busy all day and then sent into the deserted school-room with a pile of books to learn her lessons or practice at night. She had never been intimate with the other pupils, and soon she became so shabby that, taking her queer clothes together with her queer little ways, they began to look upon her as a being of another world than their own. The fact was that, as a rule, Miss Minchin's pupils were rather dull, matter-of-fact young people, accustomed to being rich and comfortable; and Sara, with her elfish cleverness, her desolate life, and her odd habit of fixing her eyes upon them and staring them out of countenance, was too much for them.

"She always looks as if she was finding you out," said one girl, who was sly and given to making mischief. "I am," said Sara promptly, when she heard of it. "That's what I look at them for. I like to know about people. I think them over afterward."

She never made any mischief herself or interfered with anyone. She talked very little, did as she was told, and thought a great deal. Nobody knew, and in fact nobody cared, whether she was unhappy or happy, unless, perhaps, it was Emily, who lived in the attic and slept on the iron bedstead at night. Sara thought Emily understood her feelings, though she was only wax and had a habit of staring herself. Sara used to talk to her at night.

"You are the only friend I have in the world," she would say to her. "Why don't you say something? Why don't you speak? Sometimes I am sure you could, if you would try. It ought to make you try, to know you are the only thing I have. If I were you, I should try. Why don't you try?"

It really was a very strange feeling she had about Emily. It arose from her being so desolate. She did not like to own to herself that her only friend, her only companion, could feel and hear nothing. She wanted to believe, or to pretend to believe, that Emily understood and sympathized with her, that she heard her even though she did not speak in answer. She used to put her in a chair sometimes and sit opposite to her on the old red footstool, and stare at her and think and pretend about her until her own eyes would grow large with something which was almost like fear, particularly at night, when the garret was so still, when the only sound that was to be heard was the occasional squeak and scurry of rats in the wainscot. There were rat-holes in the garret, and Sara detested rats, and was always glad Emily was with her when she heard their hateful squeak and rush and scratching. One of her "pretends" was that Emily was a kind of good witch and could protect her. Poor little Sara! everything was "pretend" with her. She had a strong imagination; there was almost more imagination than there was Sara, and her whole forlorn, uncared-for child-life was made up of imaginings. She imagined and pretended things until she almost believed them, and she would scarcely have been surprised at any remarkable thing that could have happened. So she insisted to herself that Emily understood all about her troubles and was really her friend.

"As to answering," she used to say, "I don't answer very often. I never answer when I can help it. When people are insulting you, there is nothing so good for them as not to say a word—just to look at them and *think*. Miss Minchin turns pale with rage when I do it. Miss Amelia looks frightened, so do the girls. They know you are stronger than they are, because you are strong enough to hold in your rage and they are not, and they say stupid things they wish they hadn't said afterward. There's nothing so strong as rage, except what makes you hold it in— that's stronger. It's a good thing not to answer your enemies. I scarcely ever do. Perhaps Emily is more like me than I am like myself. Perhaps she would rather not answer her friends, even. She keeps it all in her heart."

But though she tried to satisfy herself with these arguments, Sara did not find it easy. When, after a long, hard day, in which she had been sent here and there, sometimes on long errands, through wind and cold and rain; and, when she came in wet and hungry, had been sent out again because nobody chose to remember that she was only a child, and that her thin little legs might be tired, and her small body, clad in its forlorn, too small finery, all too short and too tight, might be chilled; when she had been given only harsh words and cold, slighting looks for thanks; when the cook had been vulgar and insolent; when Miss Minchin had been in her worst moods, and when she had seen the girls sneering at her among themselves and making fun of her poor, outgrown clothes— then Sara did not find Emily quite all that her sore, proud, desolate little heart needed as the doll sat in her little old chair and stared.

One of these nights, when she came up to the garret cold, hungry, tired, and with a tempest raging in her small breast, Emily's stare seemed so vacant, her sawdust legs and arms so limp and inexpressive, that Sara lost all control over herself.

"I shall die presently!" she said at first.

Emily stared.

"I can't bear this!" said the poor child, trembling. "I know I shall die! I'm cold, I'm wet, I'm starving to death. I've walked a thousand miles to-day, and they have done nothing but scold me from morning until night. And because I could not find that last thing they sent me for, they would not give me any supper. Some men laughed at me because my old shoes made me slip down in the mud. I'm covered with mud now. And they laughed! Do you *hear!*"

She looked at the staring glass eyes and complacent wax face, and suddenly a sort of heart-broken rage seized her. She lifted her little savage hand and knocked Emily off the chair, bursting into a passion of sobbing.

"You are nothing but a doll!" she cried. "Nothing but a doll—doll—doll! You care for nothing. You are stuffed with sawdust. You never had a heart. Nothing could ever make you feel. You are a *doll!*"

Emily lay upon the floor, with her legs ignominiously doubled up over her head, and a new flat place on the end of her nose; but she was still calm, even dignified.

Sara hid her face on her arms and sobbed. Some rats in the wall began to fight and bite each other, and squeak and scramble. But, as I have already intimated, Sara was not in the habit of crying. After a while she stopped, and when she stopped she looked at Emily, who seemed to be gazing at her around the side of one ankle, and actually with a kind of glassy-eyed sympathy. Sara bent and picked her up. Remorse overtook her.

"You can't help being a doll," she said, with a resigned sigh, "any more than those girls downstairs can help not having any sense. We are not all alike. Perhaps you do your sawdust best."

None of Miss Minchin's young ladies were very remarkable for being brilliant; they were select, but some of them were very dull, and some of them were not fond of applying themselves to their lessons. Sara, who snatched her lessons at all sorts of untimely hours from tattered and discarded books, and who had a hungry craving for everything readable, was often severe upon them in her small mind. They had books they never read; she had no books at all. If she had always had something to read, she would not have been so lonely. She liked romances and history and poetry; she would read anything. There was a sentimental housemaid in the establishment who bought the weekly penny papers, and subscribed to a circulating library, from which she got greasy volumes containing stories of marquises and dukes who invariably fell in love with orange-girls and gypsies and servant-maids, and made them the proud brides of coronets; and Sara often did parts of this maid's work so that she might earn the privilege of reading these romantic histories. There was also a fat, dull pupil, whose name was Ermengarde St. John, who was one of her resources. Ermengarde had an intellectual father, who, in his despairing desire to encourage his daughter, constantly sent her valuable and interesting books, which were a continual source of grief to her. Sara had once actually found her crying over a big package of them.

"What is the matter with you?" she asked her, perhaps rather disdainfully.

And it is just possible she would not have spoken to her, if she had not seen the books. The sight of books always gave Sara a hungry feeling, and she could not help drawing near to them if only to read their titles.

"What is the matter with you?" she asked.

"My papa has sent me some more books," answered Ermengarde woefully, "and he expects me to read them."

"Don't you like reading?" said Sara.

"I hate it!" replied Miss Ermengarde St. John. "And he will ask me questions when he sees me: he will want to know how much I remember; how would *you* like to have to read all those?"

"I'd like it better than anything else in the world," said Sara.

Ermengarde wiped her eyes to look at such a prodigy.

"Oh, gracious," she exclaimed.

Sara returned the look with interest. A sudden plan formed itself in her sharp mind.

"Look here!" she said. "If you'll lend me those books, I'll read them and tell you everything that's in them afterward, and I'll tell it to you so that you will remember it. I know I can. The A B C children always remember what I tell them."

"Oh, goodness!" said Ermengarde. "Do you think you could?"

"I know I could," answered Sara. "I like to read, and I always remember. I'll take care of the books, too; they will look just as new as they do now, when I give them back to you."

Ermengarde put her handkerchief in her pocket.

"If you'll do that," she said, "and if you'll make me remember, I'll give you—I'll give you some money."

"I don't want your money," said Sara. "I want your books—I want them." And her eyes grew big and queer, and her chest heaved once.

"Take them, then," said Ermengarde; "I wish I wanted them, but I am not clever, and my father is, and he thinks I ought to be."

Sara picked up the books and marched off with them. But when she was at the door, she stopped and turned around.

"What are you going to tell your father?" she asked.

"Oh," said Ermengarde, "he needn't know; he'll think I've read them."

Sara looked down at the books; her heart really began to beat fast.

"I won't do it," she said rather slowly, "if you are going to tell him lies about it—I don't like lies. Why can't you tell him I read them and then told you about them?"

"But he wants me to read them," said Ermengarde.

"He wants you to know what is in them," said Sara; "and if I can tell it to you in an easy way and make you remember, I should think he would like that."

"He would like it better if I read them myself," replied Ermengarde.

"He will like it, I dare say, if you learn anything in any way," said Sara. "I should, if I were your father."

And though this was not a flattering way of stating the case, Ermengarde was obliged to admit it was true, and, after a little more argument, gave in. And so she used afterward always to hand over her books to Sara, and Sara would carry them to her garret and devour them; and after she had read each volume, she would return it and tell Ermengarde about it in a way of her own. She had a gift for making things interesting. Her imagination helped her to make everything rather like a story, and she managed this matter so well that Miss St. John gained more information from her books than she would have gained if she had read them three times over by her poor stupid little self. When Sara sat down by her and began to tell some story of travel or history, she made the travellers and historical people seem real; and Ermengarde used to sit and regard her dramatic gesticulations, her thin little flushed cheeks, and her shining, odd eyes with amazement.

"It sounds nicer than it seems in the book," she would say. "I never cared about Mary, Queen of Scots, before, and I always hated the French Revolution, but you make it seem like a story."

"It is a story," Sara would answer. "They are all stories. Everything is a story—everything in this world. You are a story—I am a story—Miss Minchin is a story. You can make a story out of anything."

"I can't," said Ermengarde.

Sara stared at her a minute reflectively.

"No," she said at last. "I suppose you couldn't. You are a little like Emily."

"Who is Emily?"

Sara recollected herself. She knew she was sometimes rather impolite in the candor of her remarks, and she did not want to be impolite to a girl who was not unkind—only stupid. Notwithstanding all her sharp little ways she had the sense to wish to be just to everybody. In the hours she spent alone, she used to argue out a great many curious questions with herself. One thing she had decided upon was, that a person who was clever ought to be clever enough not to be unjust or deliberately unkind to any one.

Miss Minchin was unjust and cruel, Miss Amelia was unkind and spiteful, the cook was malicious and hasty-tempered—they all were stupid, and made her despise them, and she desired to be as unlike them as possible. So she would be as polite as she could to people who in the least deserved politeness.

"Emily is—a person—I know," she replied.

"Do you like her?" asked Ermengarde.

"Yes, I do," said Sara.

Ermengarde examined her queer little face and figure again. She did look odd. She had on, that day, a faded blue plush skirt, which barely covered her knees, a brown cloth sacque, and a pair of olive-green stockings which Miss Minchin had made her piece out with black ones, so that they would be long enough to be kept on. And yet Ermengarde was beginning slowly to admire her. Such a forlorn, thin, neglected little thing as that, who could read and read and remember and tell you things so that they did not tire you all out! A child who could speak French, who had learned German, no one knew how! One could not help staring at her and feeling interested, particularly one to whom the simplest lesson was a trouble and a woe.

"Do you like *me?*" said Ermengarde, finally, at the end of her scrutiny.

Sara hesitated one second, then she answered:

"I like you because you are not ill-natured—I like you for letting me read your books—I like you because you don't make spiteful fun of me for what I can't help. It's not your fault that——"

She pulled herself up quickly. She had been going to say, "that you are stupid."

"That what?" asked Ermengarde.

"That you can't learn things quickly. If you can't, you can't. If I can, why, I can—that's all." She paused a minute, looking at the plump face before her, and then, rather slowly, one of her wise, old-fashioned thoughts came to her.

"Perhaps," she said, "to be able to learn things quickly

isn't everything. To be kind is worth a good deal to other people. If Miss Minchin knew everything on earth, which she doesn't, and if she was like what she is now, she'd still be a detestable thing, and everybody would hate her. Lots of clever people have done harm and been wicked. Look at Robespierre——"

She stopped again and examined her companion's countenance.

"Do you remember about him?" she demanded. "I believe you've forgotten."

"Well, I don't remember *all* of it," admitted Ermengarde.

"Well," said Sara, with courage and determination, "I'll tell it to you over again."

And she plunged once more into the gory records of the French Revolution, and told such stories of it, and made such vivid pictures of its horrors, that Miss St. John was afraid to go to bed afterward, and hid her head under the blankets when she did go, and shivered until she fell asleep. But afterward she preserved lively recollections of the character of Robespierre, and did not even forget Marie Antoinette and the Princess de Lamballe.

"You know they put her head on a pike and danced around it," Sara had said; "and she had beautiful blonde hair; and when I think of her, I never see her head on her body, but always on a pike, with those furious people dancing and howling."

Yes, it was true; to this imaginative child everything was a story; and the more books she read, the more imaginative she became. One of her chief entertainments was to sit in her garret, or walk about it, and "suppose" things. On a cold night, when she had not had enough to eat, she would draw the red footstool up before the empty grate, and say in the most intense voice:

"Suppose there was a wide steel grate here, and a great glowing fire—a *glowing* fire—with beds of red-hot coal and lots of little dancing, flickering flames. Suppose there was a soft, deep rug, and this was a comfortable chair, all cushions and crimson velvet; and suppose I had a crimson velvet frock on, and a deep lace collar, like a child in a picture; and suppose all the rest of the room was furnished in lovely colors, and there were book-shelves full of books, which changed by magic as soon as you had read them; and suppose there was a little table here, with a snow-white cover on it, and little silver dishes, and in one there was hot, hot soup, and in another a roast chicken, and in another some raspberry-jam tarts with criss-cross on them, and in another some grapes; and suppose Emily could speak, and we could sit and eat our supper, and then talk and read; and then suppose there was a soft, warm bed in the corner, and when we were tired we could go to sleep, and sleep as long as we liked."

Sometimes, after she had supposed things like these for half an hour, she would feel almost warm, and would creep into bed with Emily and fall asleep with a smile on her face.

"What large, downy pillows!" she would whisper. "What white sheets and fleecy blankets!" And she almost forgot that her real pillows had scarcely any feathers in them at all, and smelled musty, and that her blankets and coverlid were thin and full of holes.

At another time she would "suppose" she was a princess, and then she would go about the house with an expression on her face which was a source of great secret annoyance to Miss Minchin, because it seemed as if the child scarcely heard the spiteful, insulting things said to her, or, if she heard them, did not care for them at all. Sometimes, while she was in the midst of some harsh and cruel speech, Miss Minchin would find the odd, unchildish eyes fixed upon her with something like a proud smile in them. At such times she did not know that Sara was saying to herself:

"You don't know that you are saying these things to a princess, and that if I chose I could wave my hand and order you to execution. I only spare you because I *am* a princess, and you are a poor, stupid, old, vulgar thing, and don't know any better."

This used to please and amuse her more than anything else; and queer and fanciful as it was, she found comfort in it, and it was not a bad thing for her. It really kept her from being made rude and malicious by the rudeness and malice of those about her.

"A princess must be polite," she said to herself. And so when the servants, who took their tone from their mistress, were insolent and ordered her about, she would hold her head erect, and reply to them sometimes in a way which made them stare at her, it was so quaintly civil.

"I am a princess in rags and tatters," she would think, "but I am a princess, inside. It would be easy to be a princess if I were dressed in cloth-of-gold; it is a great deal more of a triumph to be one all the time when no one knows it. There was Marie Antoinette: when she was in prison, and her throne was gone, and she had only a black gown on, and her hair was white, and they insulted her and called her the Widow Capet,—she was a great deal more like a queen then than when she was so gay and had everything grand. I like her best then. Those howling mobs of people did not frighten her. She was stronger than they were even when they cut her head off."

Once when such thoughts were passing through her mind the look in her eyes so enraged Miss Minchin that she flew at Sara and boxed her ears.

Sara awakened from her dream, started a little, and then broke into a laugh.

"What are you laughing at, you bold, impudent child!" exclaimed Miss Minchin.

It took Sara a few seconds to remember she was a princess. Her cheeks were red and smarting from the blows she had received.

"I was thinking," she said.

"Beg my pardon immediately," said Miss Minchin.

"I will beg your pardon for laughing, if it was rude," said Sara; "but I won't beg your pardon for thinking."

"What were you thinking?" demanded Miss Minchin. "How dare you think? What were you thinking?"

This occurred in the school-room, and all the girls looked up from their books to listen. It always interested them when Miss Minchin flew at Sara, because Sara always said something queer, and never seemed in the least frightened. She was not in the least frightened now, though her boxed ears were scarlet, and her eyes were as bright as stars.

"I was thinking," she answered gravely and quite politely, "that you did not know what you were doing."

"That I did not know what I was doing!" Miss Minchin fairly gasped.

"Yes," said Sara, "and I was thinking what would happen, if I were a princess and you boxed my ears—what I should do to you. And I was thinking that if I were one, you would never dare to do it, whatever I said or did. And I was thinking how surprised and frightened you would be if you suddenly found out——"

She had the imagined picture so clearly before her eyes, that she spoke in a manner which had an effect even on Miss Minchin. It almost seemed for the moment to her narrow, unimaginative mind that there must be some real power behind this candid daring.

"What!" she exclaimed, "found out what?"

"That I really was a princess," said Sara, "and could do anything—anything I liked."

"Go to your room," cried Miss Minchin breathlessly, "this instant. Leave the school-room. Attend to your lessons, young ladies."

Sara made a little bow.

"Excuse me for laughing, if it was impolite," she said, and walked out of the room, leaving Miss Minchin in a rage and the girls whispering over their books.

"I shouldn't be at all surprised if she did turn out to be something," said one of them. "Suppose she should!"

That very afternoon Sara had an opportunity of proving to herself whether she was really a princess or not. It was a dreadful afternoon. For several days it had rained continuously, the streets were chilly and sloppy; there was mud everywhere—sticky London mud—and over everything a pall of fog and drizzle. Of course there were several long and tiresome errands to be done,—there always were on days like this,—and Sara was sent out again and again, until her shabby clothes were damp through. The absurd old feathers on her forlorn hat were more draggled and absurd than ever, and her down-trodden shoes were so wet they could not hold any more water. Added to this, she had been deprived of her dinner, because Miss Minchin wished to punish her. She was very hungry. She was so cold and hungry and tired that her little face had a pinched look, and now and then some kind-hearted person passing her in the crowded street glanced at her with sympathy. But she did not know that. She hurried on, trying to comfort herself in that queer way of hers by pretending and "supposing,"—but really this time it was harder than she had ever found it, and once or twice she thought it almost made her more cold and hungry instead of less so. But she persevered obsti-nately. "Suppose I had dry clothes on," she thought. "Suppose I had good shoes and a long, thick coat and merino stockings and a whole umbrella. And suppose—suppose, just when I was near a baker's where they sold hot buns, I should find sixpence—which belonged to nobody. Suppose, if I did, I should go into the shop and buy six of the hottest buns, and should eat them all without stopping."

Some very odd things happen in this world sometimes. It certainly was an odd thing which happened to Sara. She had to cross the street just as she was saying this to her-self—the mud was dreadful—she almost had to wade. She picked her way as carefully as she could, but she could not save herself much, only, in picking her way she had to look down at her feet and the mud, and in look-ing down—just as she reached the pavement—she saw something shining in the gutter. A piece of silver—a tiny piece trodden upon by many feet, but still with spirit enough to shine a little. Not quite a sixpence, but the next thing to it—a four-penny piece! In one second it was in her cold, little red and blue hand.

"Oh!" she gasped. "It is true!"

And then, if you will believe me, she looked straight before her at the shop directly facing her. And it was a baker's, and a cheerful, stout, motherly woman, with rosy cheeks, was just putting into the window a tray of delicious hot buns,—large, plump, shiny buns, with currants in them.

It almost made Sara feel faint for a few seconds— the shock and the sight of the buns and the delightful odors of warm bread floating up through the baker's cellar-window.

She knew that she need not hesitate to use the little piece of money. It had evidently been lying in the mud for some time, and its owner was completely lost in the streams of passing people who crowded and jostled each other all through the day.

"But I'll go and ask the baker's woman if she has lost a piece of money," she said to herself, rather faintly.

So she crossed the pavement and put her wet foot on the step of the shop; and as she did so she saw something which made her stop.

It was a little figure more forlorn than her own—a little figure which was not much more than a bundle of rags, from which small, bare, red and muddy feet peeped out— only because the rags with which the wearer was trying to cover them were not long enough. Above the rags appeared a shock head of tangled hair and a dirty face, with big, hollow, hungry eyes.

Sara knew they were hungry eyes the moment she saw them, and she felt a sudden sympathy.

"This," she said to herself, with a little sigh, "is one of the Populace—and she is hungrier than I am."

The child—this "one of the Populace"—stared up at Sara, and shuffled herself aside a little, so as to give her more room. She was used to being made to give room to everybody. She knew that if a policeman chanced to see her, he would tell her to "move on."

Sara clutched her little four-penny piece, and hesitated a few seconds. Then she spoke to her.

"Are you hungry?" she asked.

The child shuffled herself and her rags a little more.

"Ain't I jist!" she said, in a hoarse voice. "Jist ain't I!"

"Haven't you had any dinner?" said Sara.

"No dinner," more hoarsely still and with more shuffling, "nor yet no bre'fast—nor yet no supper—nor nothin'."

"Since when?" asked Sara.

"Dun'no. Never got nothin' to-day—nowhere. I've axed and axed."

Just to look at her made Sara more hungry and faint. But those queer little thoughts were at work in her brain, and she was talking to herself though she was sick at heart.

"If I'm a princess," she was saying—"if I'm a princess—! When they were poor and driven from their thrones— they always shared—with the Populace—if they met one poorer and hungrier. They always shared. Buns are a penny each. If it had been sixpence! I could have eaten six. It won't be enough for either of us—but it will be better than nothing."

"Wait a minute," she said to the beggar-child. She went into the shop. It was warm and smelled delightfully. The woman was just going to put more hot buns in the window.

"If you please," said Sara, "have you lost fourpence—a silver fourpence?" And she held the forlorn little piece of money out to her.

The woman looked at it and at her—at her intense little face and draggled, once-fine clothes.

"Bless us—no," she answered. "Did you find it?"

"In the gutter," said Sara.

"Keep it then," said the woman. "It may have been there

a week, and goodness knows who lost it. *You* could never find out."

"I know that," said Sara, "but I thought 'd ask you."

"Not many would," said the woman, looking puzzled and interested and good-natured all at once. "Do you want to buy something?" she added, as she saw Sara glance toward the buns.

"Four buns, if you please," said Sara; "those at a penny each."

The woman went to the window and put some in a paper bag. Sara noticed that she put in six.

"I said four, if you please," she explained. "I have only the fourpence.'

"I'll throw in two for make-weight," said the woman, with her good-natured look. "I dare say you can eat them some time. Aren't you hungry?"

A mist rose before Sara's eyes.

"Yes," she answered. "I am very hungry, and I am much obliged to you for your kindness, and," she was going to add, "there is a child outside who is hungrier than I am." But just at that moment two or three customers came in at once and each one seemed in a hurry, so she could only thank the woman again and go out.

The child was still huddled up on the corner of the steps. She looked frightful in her wet and dirty rags. She was staring with a stupid look of suffering straight before her, and Sara saw her suddenly draw the back of her roughened, black hand across her eyes to rub away the tears which seemed to have surprised her by forcing their way from under her lids. She was muttering to herself.

Sara opened the paper bag and took out one of the hot buns, which had already warmed her cold hands a little.

"See," she said, putting the bun on the ragged lap, "that is nice and hot. Eat it, and you will not be so hungry."

The child started and stared up at her; then she snatched up the bun and began to cram it into her mouth with great wolfish bites.

"Oh, my! Oh, my!" Sara heard her say hoarsely, in wild delight.

"Oh, my!"

Sara took out three more buns and put them down.

"She is hungrier than I am," she said to her herself. "She's starving." But her hand trembled when she put down the fourth bun. "I'm not starving," she said—and she put down the fifth.

The little starving London savage was still snatching and devouring when she turned away. She was too ravenous to give any thanks, even if she had been taught politeness—which she had not. She was only a poor little wild animal.

"Good-bye," said Sara.

When she reached the other side of the street she looked back. The child had a bun in both hands, and had stopped in the middle of a bite to watch her. Sara gave her a little nod, and the child, after another stare,—a curious, longing stare,—jerked her shaggy head in response, and until Sara was out of sight she did not take another bite or even finish the one she had begun.

At that moment the baker-woman glanced out of her shop-window.

"Well, I never!" she exclaimed. "If that young 'un hasn't given her buns to a beggar-child! It wasn't because she didn't want them, either—well, well, she looked hungry enough. I'd give something to know what she did it for." She stood behind her window for a few moments and pondered. Then her curiosity got the better of her. She went to the door and spoke to the beggar-child.

"Who gave you those buns?" she asked her.

The child nodded her head toward Sara's vanishing figure.

"What did she say?" inquired the woman.

"Axed me if I was 'ungry," replied the hoarse voice.

"What did you say?"

"Said I was jist!"

"And then she came in and got buns and came out and gave them to you, did she?"

The child nodded.

"How many?"

"Five."

The woman thought it over. "Left just one for herself," she said, in a low voice. "And she could have eaten the whole six—I saw it in her eyes."

She looked after the little, draggled, far-away figure, and felt more disturbed in her usually comfortable mind than she had felt for many a day.

"I wish she hadn't gone so quick," she said. "I'm blest if she shouldn't have had a dozen."

Then she turned to the child.

"Are you hungry, yet?" she asked.

"I'm allus 'ungry," was the answer; "but 'tain't so bad as it was."

"Come in here," said the woman, and she held open the shop-door.

The child got up and shuffled in. To be invited into a warm place full of bread seemed an incredible thing. She did not know what was going to happen; she did not care, even.

"Get yourself warm," said the woman, pointing to a fire in a tiny back room. "And, look here,—when you're hard up for a bite of bread, you can come here and ask for it. I'm blest if I won't give it to you for that young un's sake."

Sara found some comfort in her remaining bun. It was hot; and it was a great deal better than nothing. She broke off small pieces and ate them slowly to make it last longer.

"Suppose it was a magic bun," she said, "and a bite was as much as a whole dinner. I should be over-eating myself if I went on like this."

It was dark when she reached the square in which Miss Minchin's Select Seminary was situated; the lamps were lighted, and in most of the windows gleams of light were to be seen. It always interested Sara to catch glimpses of the rooms before the shutters were closed. She liked to imagine things about people who sat before the fires in the houses, or who bent over books at the tables. There was, for instance, the Large Family opposite. She called these people the Large Family—not because they were large, for indeed most of them were little,—but because there were so many of them. There were eight children in the Large Family, and a stout, rosy mother, and a stout, rosy father, and a stout, rosy grandmamma, and any number of servants. The eight children were always either being taken out to walk, or to ride in perambulators, by comfortable nurses; or they were going to drive with their mamma; or they were flying to the door in the evening to kiss their papa and dance around him and drag off his overcoat and look for packages in the pockets of it; or they were crowding about the nursery windows and looking out and pushing each other and laughing,—in fact they were always doing something which seemed enjoyable and suited to the tastes of a large family. Sara was quite attached to them, and had given them all names out of books. She called them the Montmorencys, when she did not call them the Large Family. The fat, fair baby with the lace cap was Ethelberta Beauchamp Montmorency; the next baby was Violet Cholmondely Montmorency; the little boy who could just stagger, and who had such round legs, was Sydney Cecil Vivian Montmorency; and then came Lilian Evangeline, Guy Clarence, Maud Marian, Rosalind Gladys, Veronica Eustacia, and Claude Harold Hector.

Next door to the Large Family lived the Maiden Lady, who had a companion, and two parrots, and a King Charles spaniel; but Sara was not so very fond of her, because she did nothing in particular but talk to the parrots and drive out with the spaniel. The most interesting person of all lived next door to Miss Minchin herself. Sara called him the Indian Gentleman. He was an elderly gentleman who was said to have lived in the East Indies, and to be immensely rich and to have something the matter with his liver,—in fact, it had been rumored that he had no liver at all, and was much inconvenienced by the fact.

At any rate, he was very yellow and he did not look happy; and when he went out to his carriage, he was almost always wrapped up in shawls and overcoats, as if he were cold. He had a native servant who looked even colder than himself, and he had a monkey who looked colder than the native servant. Sara had seen the monkey sitting on a table, in the sun, in the parlor window, and he always wore such a mournful expression that she sympathized with him deeply.

"I dare say," she used sometimes to remark to herself, "he is thinking all the time of cocoanut trees and of swinging by his tail under a tropical sun. He might have had a family dependent on him too, poor thing!"

The native servant, whom she called the Lascar, looked mournful too, but he was evidently very faithful to his master.

"Perhaps he saved his master's life in the Sepoy rebellion," she thought. "They look as if they might have had all sorts of adventures. I wish I could speak to the Lascar. I remember a little Hindustani."

And one day she actually did speak to him, and his start at the sound of his own language expressed a great deal of surprise and delight. He was waiting for his master to come out to the carriage, and Sara, who was going on an errand as usual, stopped and spoke a few words. She had a special gift for languages and had remembered enough Hindustani to make herself understood by him. When his master came out, the Lascar spoke to him quickly, and the Indian Gentleman turned and looked at her curiously. And afterward the Lascar always greeted her with salaams of the most profound description. And occasionally they exchanged a few words. She learned that it was true that the Sahib was very rich—that he was ill—and also that he had no wife nor children, and that England did not agree with the monkey.

"He must be as lonely as I am," thought Sara. "Being rich does not seem to make him happy."

That evening, as she passed the windows, the Lascar

was closing the shutters, and she caught a glimpse of the room inside. There was a bright fire glowing in the grate, and the Indian Gentleman was sitting before it, in a luxurious chair. The room was richly furnished, and looked delightfully comfortable, but the Indian Gentleman sat with his head resting on his hand, and looked as lonely and unhappy as ever.

"Poor man!" said Sara; "I wonder what *you* are 'supposing'?"

When she went into the house she met Miss Minchin in the hall.

"Where have you wasted your time?" said Miss Minchin. "You have been out for hours!"

"It was so wet and muddy," Sara answered. "It was hard to walk, because my shoes were so bad and slipped about so."

"Make no excuses," said Miss Minchin, "and tell no falsehoods."

Sara went downstairs to the kitchen.

"Why didn't you stay all night?" said the cook.

"Here are the things," said Sara, and laid her purchases on the table.

The cook looked over them, grumbling. She was in a very bad temper indeed.

"May I have something to eat?" Sara asked rather faintly.

"Tea's over and done with," was the answer. "Did you expect me to keep it hot for you?"

Sara was silent a second.

"I had no dinner," she said, and her voice was quite low. She made it low, because she was afraid it would tremble.

"There's some bread in the pantry," said the cook. "That's all you'll get at this time of day."

Sara went and found the bread. It was old and hard and dry. The cook was in too bad a humor to give her anything to eat with it. She had just been scolded by Miss Minchin, and it was always safe and easy to vent her own spite on Sara.

Really it was hard for the child to climb the three long flights of stairs leading to her garret. She often found them long and steep when she was tired, but to-night it seemed as if she would never reach the top. Several times a lump rose in her throat and she was obliged to stop to rest.

"I can't pretend anything more to-night," she said wearily to herself. "I'm sure I can't. I'll eat my bread and drink some water and then go to sleep, and perhaps a dream will come and pretend for me. I wonder what dreams are."

Yes, when she reached the top landing there were tears in her eyes, and she did not feel like a princess—only like a tired, hungry, lonely, lonely child.

"If my papa had lived," she said, "they would not have treated me like this. If my papa had lived, he would have taken care of me."

Then she turned the handle and opened the garret-door.

Can you imagine it—can you believe it? I find it hard to believe it myself. And Sara found it impossible; for the first few moments she thought something strange had happened to her eyes—to her mind—that the dream had come before she had had time to fall asleep.

"Oh!" she exclaimed breathlessly. "Oh! It isn't true! I know, I know it isn't true!" And she slipped into the room and closed the door and locked it, and stood with her back against it, staring straight before her.

Do you wonder? In the grate, which had been empty and rusty and cold when she left it, but which now was blackened and polished up quite respectably, there was a glowing, blazing fire. On the hob was a little brass kettle, hissing and boiling; spread upon the floor was a warm, thick rug; before the fire was a folding-chair, unfolded and with cushions on it; by the chair was a small folding-table, unfolded, covered with a white cloth, and upon it were spread small covered dishes, a cup and saucer, and a tea-pot; on the bed were new, warm coverings, a curious wadded silk robe, and some books. The little, cold, miserable room seemed changed into Fairyland. It was actually warm and glowing.

"It is bewitched!" said Sara. "Or *I* am bewitched. I only *think* I see it all; but if I can only keep on thinking it, I don't care—I don't care—if I can only keep it up!"

She was afraid to move, for fear it would melt away. She stood with her back against the door and looked and looked. But soon she began to feel warm, and then she moved forward.

"A fire that I only *thought* I saw surely wouldn't *feel* warm," she said. "It feels real—real."

She went to it and knelt before it. She touched the chair, the table; she lifted the cover of one of the dishes. There was something hot and savory in it—something delicious. The tea-pot had tea in it, ready for the boiling water from the little kettle; one plate had toast on it, another, muffins.

"It is real," said Sara. "The fire is real enough to warm me; I can sit in the chair; the things are real enough to eat."

It was like a fairy story come true—it was heavenly. She went to bed and touched the blankets and the wrap. They were real too. She opened one book, and on the title-page was written in a strange hand, "The little girl in the attic."

Suddenly—was it a strange thing for her to do?—Sara put her face down on the queer, foreign looking quilted robe and burst into tears.

"I don't know who it is," she said, "but somebody cares about me a little—somebody is my friend."

Somehow that thought warmed her more than the fire. She had never had a friend since those happy, luxurious days when she had had everything; and those days had seemed such a long way off—so far away as to be only like dreams—during these last years at Miss Minchin's.

She really cried more at this strange thought of having a friend—even though an unknown one—than she had cried over many of her worst troubles.

But these tears seemed different from the others, for when she had wiped them away they did not seem to leave her eyes and her heart hot and smarting.

And then imagine, if you can, what the rest of the

evening was like. The delicious comfort of taking off the damp clothes and putting on the soft, warm, quilted robe before the glowing fire—of slipping her cold feet into the luscious little wool-lined slippers she found near her chair. And then the hot tea and savory dishes, the cushioned chair and the books!

It was just like Sara, that, once having found the things real, she should give herself up to the enjoyment of them to the very utmost. She had lived such a life of imagining, and had found her pleasure so long in improbabilities, that she was quite equal to accepting any wonderful thing that happened. After she was quite warm and had eaten her supper and enjoyed herself for an hour or so, it had almost ceased to be surprising to her that such magical surroundings should be hers. As to finding out who had done all this, she knew that it was out of the question. She did not know a human soul by whom it could seem in the least degree probable that it could have been done.

"There is nobody," she said to herself, "Nobody." She discussed the matter with Emily, it is true, but more because it was delightful to talk about it than with a view to making any discoveries.

"But we have a friend, Emily," she said; "we have a friend."

Sara could not even imagine a being charming enough to fill her grand ideal of her mysterious benefactor. If she tried to make in her mind a picture of him or her, it ended by being something glittering and strange—not at all like a real person, but bearing resemblance to a sort of Eastern magician, with long robes and a wand. And when she fell asleep, beneath the soft white blanket, she dreamed all night of this magnificent personage, and talked to him in Hindustani, and made salaams to him.

Upon one thing she was determined. She would not speak to any one of her good fortune—it should be her own secret; in fact, she was rather inclined to think that if Miss Minchin knew, she would take her treasures from her or in some way spoil her pleasure. So, when she went down the next morning, she shut her door very tight and did her best to look as if nothing unusual had occurred. And yet this was rather hard, because she could not help remembering, every now and then, with a sort of start, and her heart would beat quickly every time she repeated to herself, "I have a friend!"

It was a friend who evidently meant to continue to be kind, for when she went to her garret the next night—and she opened the door, it must be confessed, with rather an excited feeling—she found that the same hands had been again at work, and had done even more than before. The fire and the supper were again there, and beside them a number of other things which so altered the look of the garret that Sara quite lost her breath. A piece of bright, strange, heavy cloth covered the battered mantel, and on it some ornaments had been placed. All the bare, ugly things which could be covered with draperies had been concealed and made to look quite pretty. Some odd materials in rich colors had been fastened against the walls with sharp, fine tacks—so sharp that they could be pressed into the wood without hammering. Some brilliant fans were pinned up, and there were several large cushions. A long, old wooden box was covered with a rug, and some cushions lay on it, so that it wore quite the air of a sofa.

Sara simply sat down, and looked, and looked again.

"It is exactly like something fairy come true," she said; "there isn't the least difference. I feel as if I might wish for anything—diamonds and bags of gold—and they would appear! *That* couldn't be any stranger than this. Is this my garret? Am I the same cold, ragged, damp Sara? And to think how I used to pretend, and pretend, and wish there were fairies! The one thing I always wanted was to see a fairy story come true. I am *living* in a fairy story! I feel as if I might be a fairy myself, and be able to turn things into anything else!"

It was like a fairy story, and, what was best of all, it continued. Almost every day something new was done to the garret. Some new comfort or ornament appeared in it when Sara opened her door at night, until actually, in a short time, it was a bright little room full of all sorts of odd and luxurious things. And the magician had taken care that the child should not be hungry, and that she should have as many books as she could read. When she left the room in the morning, the remains of her supper were on the table, and when she returned in the evening, the magician had removed them, and left another nice little meal. Downstairs Miss Minchin was as cruel and insulting as ever, Miss Amelia was as peevish, and the servants were as vulgar. Sara was sent on errands, and scolded, and driven hither and thither, but somehow it seemed as if she could bear it all. The delightful sense of romance and mystery lifted her above the cook's temper and malice. The comfort she enjoyed and could always look forward to was making her stronger. If she came home from her errands wet and tired, she knew she would soon be warm, after she had climbed the stairs. In a few weeks she began to look less thin. A little color came into her cheeks, and her eyes did not seem much too big for her face.

It was just when this was beginning to be so apparent that Miss Minchin sometimes stared at her questioningly, that another wonderful thing happened. A man came to the door and left several parcels. All were addressed (in large letters) to "the little girl in the attic." Sara herself was sent to open the door, and she took them in. She laid the two largest parcels down on the hall-table and was looking at the address, when Miss Minchin came down the stairs.

"Take the things upstairs to the young lady to whom they belong," she said. "Don't stand there staring at them."

"They belong to me," answered Sara, quietly.

"To you!" exclaimed Miss Minchin. "What do you mean?"

"I don't know where they came from," said Sara, "but they're addressed to me."

Miss Minchin came to her side and looked at them with an excited expression.

"What is in them?" she demanded.

"I don't know," said Sara.

"Open them!" she demanded, still more excitedly.

Sara did as she was told. They contained pretty and comfortable clothing,—clothing of different kinds; shoes and stockings and gloves, a warm coat, and even an umbrella. On the pocket of the coat was pinned a paper on which was written, "To be worn every day—will be replaced by others when necessary."

Miss Minchin was quite agitated. This was an incident which suggested strange things to her sordid mind. Could it be that she had made a mistake after all, and that the child so neglected and so unkindly treated by her had some powerful friend in the background? It would not be very pleasant if there should be such a friend, and he or she should learn all the truth about the thin, shabby clothes, the scant food, the hard work. She felt queer indeed and uncertain, and she gave a side-glance at Sara.

"Well," she said, in a voice such as she had never used since the day the child lost her father—"well, some one is very kind to you. As you have the things and are to have new ones when they are worn out, you may as well go and put them on and look respectable; and after you are dressed, you may come downstairs and learn your lessons in the school-room."

So it happened that, about half an hour afterward, Sara struck the entire school-room of pupils dumb with amazement, by making her appearance in a costume such as she had never worn since the change of fortune whereby she ceased to be a show-pupil and a parlor-boarder. She scarcely seemed to be the same Sara. She was neatly dressed in a pretty gown of warm browns and reds, and even her stockings and slippers were nice and dainty.

"Perhaps some one has left her a fortune," one of the

girls whispered. "I always thought something would happen to her, she is so queer."

That night when Sara went to her room she carried out a plan she had been devising for some time. She wrote a note to her unknown friend. It ran as follows:

"I hope you will not think it is not polite that I should write this note to you when you wish to keep yourself a secret, but I do not mean to be impolite, or to try to find out at all, only I want to thank you for being so kind to me—so beautiful kind, and making everything like a fairy story. I am so grateful to you and I am so happy! I used to be so lonely and cold and, hungry, and now, oh, just think what you have done for me! Please let me say just these words. It seems as if I ought to say them. *Thank you—thank you—thank you!*

"THE LITTLE GIRL IN THE ATTIC."

The next morning she left this on the little table, and it was taken away with the other things; so she felt sure the magician had received it, and she was happier for the thought.

A few nights later a very odd thing happened. She found something in the room which she certainly would never have expected. When she came in as usual she saw something small and dark in her chair,—an odd, tiny figure, which turned toward her a little, weird-looking, wistful face.

"Why, it's the monkey!" she cried. "It is the Indian Gentleman's monkey! Where can he have come from?"

It *was* the monkey, sitting up and looking so like a mite of a child that it really was quite pathetic; and very soon Sara found out how he happened to be in her room. The skylight was open, and it was easy to guess that he had crept out of his master's garret-window, which was only a few feet away and perfectly easy to get in and out of, even for a climber less agile than a monkey. He had probably climbed to the garret on a tour of investigation, and getting out upon the roof, and being attracted by the light in

Sara's attic, had crept in. At all events this seemed quite reasonable, and there he was; and when Sara went to him, he actually put out his queer, elfish little hands, caught her dress, and jumped into her arms.

"Oh, you queer, poor, ugly, foreign little thing!" said Sara, caressing him. "I can't help liking you. You look like a sort of baby, but I am so glad you are not, because your mother could *not* be proud of you, and nobody would dare to say you were like any of your relations. But I do like you; you have such a forlorn little look in your face. Perhaps you are sorry you are so ugly, and it's always on your mind. I wonder if you have a mind?"

The monkey sat and looked at her while she talked, and seemed much interested in her remarks, if one could judge by his eyes and his forehead, and the way he moved his head up and down, and held it sideways and scratched it with his little hand. He examined Sara quite seriously, and anxiously, too. He felt the stuff of her dress, touched her hands, climbed up and examined her ears, and then sat on her shoulder holding a lock of her hair, looking mournful but not at all agitated. Upon the whole, he seemed pleased with Sara.

"But I must take you back," she said to him, "though I'm sorry to have to do it. Oh, the company you *would* be to a person!"

She lifted him from her shoulder, set him on her knee, and gave him a bit of cake. He sat and nibbled it, and then put his head on one side, looked at her, wrinkled his forehead, and then nibbled again, in the most companionable manner.

"But you must go home," said Sara at last; and she took him in her arms to carry him downstairs. Evidently he did not want to leave the room, for as they reached the door he clung to her neck and gave a little scream of anger.

"You mustn't be an ungrateful monkey," said Sara. "You ought to be fondest of your own family. I am sure the Lascar is good to you."

Nobody saw her on her way out, and very soon she was

standing on the Indian Gentleman's front steps, and the Lascar had opened the door for her.

"I found your monkey in my room," she said in Hindustani. "I think he got in through the window."

The man began a rapid outpouring of thanks; but, just as he was in the midst of them, a fretful, hollow voice was heard through the open door of the nearest room. The instant he heard it the Lascar disappeared, and left Sara still holding the monkey.

It was not many moments, however, before he came back bringing a message. His master had told him to bring Missy into the library. The Sahib was very ill, but he wished to see Missy.

Sara thought this odd, but she remembered reading stories of Indian gentlemen who, having no constitutions, were extremely cross and full of whims, and who must have their own way. So she followed the Lascar.

When she entered the room the Indian Gentleman was lying on an easy chair, propped up with pillows. He looked frightfully ill. His yellow face was thin, and his eyes were hollow. He gave Sara a rather curious look—it was as if she wakened in him some anxious interest.

"You live next door?" he said.

"Yes," answered Sara. "I live at Miss Minchin's."

"She keeps a boarding-school?"

"Yes," said Sara.

"And you are one of her pupils?"

Sara hesitated a moment.

"I don't know exactly what I am," she replied.

"Why not?" asked the Indian Gentleman.

The monkey gave a tiny squeak, and Sara stroked him.

"At first," she said, "I was a pupil and a parlor boarder; but now——"

"What do you mean by 'at first'?" asked the Indian Gentleman.

"When I was first taken there by my papa."

"Well, what has happened since then?" said the invalid,

staring at her and knitting his brows with a puzzled expression.

"My papa died," said Sara. "He lost all his money, and there was none left for me—and there was no one to take care of me or pay Miss Minchin, so——"

"So you were sent up into the garret and neglected, and made into a half-starved little drudge!" put in the Indian Gentleman. "That is about it, isn't it?"

The color deepened on Sara's cheeks.

"There was no one to take care of me, and no money," she said. "I belong to nobody."

"What did your father mean by losing his money?" said the gentleman, fretfully.

The red in Sara's cheeks grew deeper, and she fixed her odd eyes on the yellow face.

"He did not lose it himself," she said. "He had a friend he was fond of, and it was his friend who took his money. I don't know how. I don't understand. He trusted his friend too much."

She saw the invalid start—the strangest start—as if he had been suddenly frightened. Then he spoke nervously and excitedly:

"That's an old story," he said. "It happens every day; but sometimes those who are blamed—those who do the wrong—don't intend it, and are not so bad. It may happen through a mistake—a miscalculation; they may not be so bad."

"No," said Sara, "but the suffering is just as bad for the others. It killed my papa."

The Indian Gentleman pushed aside some of the gorgeous wraps that covered him.

"Come a little nearer, and let me look at you," he said.

His voice sounded very strange; it had a more nervous and excited tone than before. Sara had an odd fancy that he was half afraid to look at her. She came and stood nearer, the monkey clinging to her and watching his master anxiously over his shoulder.

The Indian Gentleman's hollow, restless eyes fixed themselves on her.

"Yes," he said at last. "Yes; I can see it. Tell me your father's name."

"His name was Ralph Crewe," said Sara. "Captain Crewe. Perhaps,"—a sudden thought flashing upon her,—"perhaps you may have heard of him? He died in India."

The Indian Gentleman sank back upon his pillows. He looked very weak, and seemed out of breath.

"Yes," she said, "I knew him. I was his friend. I meant no harm. If he had only lived he would have known. It turned out well after all. He was a fine young fellow. I was fond of him. I will make it right. Call—call the man."

Sara thought he was going to die. But there was no need to call the Lascar. He must have been waiting at the door. He was in the room and by his master's side in an instant. He seemed to know what to do. He lifted the drooping head, and gave the invalid something in a small glass. The Indian Gentleman lay panting for a few minutes, and then he spoke in an exhausted but eager voice, addressing the Lascar in Hindustani:

"Go for Carmichael," he said. "Tell him to come here at once. Tell him I have found the child!"

When Mr. Carmichael arrived (which occurred in a very few minutes, for it turned out that he was no other than the father of the Large Family across the street), Sara went home, and was allowed to take the monkey with her. She certainly did not sleep very much that night, though the monkey behaved beautifully, and did not disturb her in the least. It was not the monkey that kept her awake—it was her thoughts, and her wonders as to what the Indian Gentleman had meant when he said, "Tell him I have found the child." "What child?" Sara kept asking herself. "I was the only child there; but how had he found me, and why did he want to find me? And what is he going to do, now I am found? Is it something about my papa? Do I belong to somebody? Is he one of my relations? Is something going to happen?"

But she found out the very next day, in the morning; and it seemed that she had been living in a story even more than she had imagined. First, Mr. Carmichael came and had an interview with Miss Minchin. And it appeared that Mr. Carmichael, besides occupying the important situation of father to the Large Family was a lawyer, and had charge of the affairs of Mr. Carrisford—which was the real name of the Indian Gentleman—and, as Mr. Carrisford's lawyer, Mr. Carmichael had come to explain something curious to Miss Minchin regarding Sara. But, being the father of the Large Family, he had a very kind and fatherly feeling for children; and so, after seeing Miss Minchin alone, what did he do but go and bring across the square his rosy, motherly, warm-hearted wife, so that she herself might talk to the little lonely girl, and tell her everything in the best and most motherly way.

And then Sara learned that she was to be a poor little drudge and outcast no more; and that a great change had come in her fortunes; for all the lost fortune had come back to her, and a great deal had even been added to it. It was Mr. Carrisford who had been her father's friend, and who had made the investments which had caused him the apparent loss of his money; but it had so happened that after poor young Captain Crewe's death one of the investments which had seemed at the time the very worst had taken a sudden turn, and proved to be such a success that it had been a mine of wealth, and had more than doubled the Captain's lost fortune, as well as making a fortune for Mr. Carrisford himself. But Mr. Carrisford had been very unhappy. He had truly loved his poor, handsome, generous young friend, and the knowledge that he had caused his death had weighed upon him always, and broken both his health and spirit. The worst of it had been that, when first he thought himself and Captain Crewe ruined, he had lost courage and gone away because he was not brave enough to face the consequences of what he had done, and so he had not even known where the young soldier's little girl had been placed. When he wanted to find her, and make restitution, he could discover no trace of her; and the certainty that she was poor and friendless somewhere had made him more miserable than ever. When he had taken the house next to Miss Minchin's he had been so ill and wretched that he had for the time given up the search. His troubles and the Indian climate had brought him almost to death's door—indeed, he had not expected to live more than a few months. And then one day the Lascar had told him about Sara's speaking Hindustani, and gradually he had begun to take a sort of interest in the forlorn child, though he had only caught a glimpse of her once or twice and he had not connected her with the child of his friend, perhaps because he was too languid to think much about anything. But the Lascar had found out something of Sara's unhappy little life, and about the garret. One evening he had actually crept out of his own garret-window and looked into hers, which was a very easy matter, because, as I have said, it was only a few feet away—and he had told his master what he had seen, and in a moment of compassion the Indian Gentleman had told him to take into the wretched little room such comforts as he could carry from the one window to the other. And the Lascar, who had developed an interest in, and an odd fondness for, the child who had spoken to him in his own tongue, had been pleased with the work; and, having the silent swiftness and agile movements of many of his race, he had made his evening journeys across the few feet of roof from garret-window to garret-window, without any trouble at all. He had watched Sara's movements until he knew exactly when she was absent from her room and when she returned to it, and so he had been able to calculate the best times for his work. Generally he had made them in the dusk of the evening; but once or twice, when he had seen her go out on errands, he had dared to go over in the daytime, being quite sure that the garret was never entered by anyone but herself. His pleasure in the work and his reports of the results had added to the invalid's interest in it, and sometimes the master had found the planning gave him something to think of, which made him almost forget his weariness and pain. And at last, when Sara brought home the truant monkey, he had felt a wish to see her, and then her likeness to her father had done the rest.

"And now, my dear," said good Mrs. Carmichael, patting Sara's hand, "all your troubles are over, I am sure, and you are to come home with me and be taken care of as if you were one of my own little girls; and we are so pleased to think of having you with us until everything is settled, and Mr. Carrisford is better. The excitement of last night has made him very weak, but we really think he will get well, now that such a load is taken from his mind. And when he is stronger, I am sure he will be as kind to you as your own papa would have been. He has a very good heart, and he is fond of children—and he has no family at all. But we must make you happy and rosy, and you must learn to play and run about, as my little girls do——"

"As your little girls do?" said Sara. "I wonder if I could. I used to watch them and wonder what it was like. Shall I feel as if I belonged to somebody?"

"Ah, my love, yes!—yes!" said Mrs. Carmichael; "dear me, yes!" And her motherly blue eyes grew quite moist, and she suddenly took Sara in her arms and kissed her. That very night, before she went to sleep, Sara had made the acquaintance of the entire Large Family, and such excitement as she and the monkey had caused in that joyous circle could hardly be described. There was not a child in the nursery, from the Eton boy who was the eldest, to the baby who was the youngest, who had not laid some offering on her shrine. All the older ones knew something of her wonderful story. She had been born in India; she had been poor and lonely and unhappy, and had lived in a garret and been treated unkindly; and now she was to be rich and happy, and be taken of. They were so sorry for her, and so delighted and curious about her, all at once. The girls wished to be with her constantly, and the little boys wished to be told about India; the second baby, with the short round legs, simply sat and stared at her and the monkey, possibly wondering why she had not brought a hand-organ with her.

"I shall certainly wake up presently," Sara kept saying to herself. "This one must be a dream. The other one turned out to be real; but this *couldn't* be. But, oh! how happy it is!"

And even when she went to bed, in the bright, pretty room not far from Mrs. Carmichael's own, and Mrs. Carmichael came and kissed her and patted her and tucked her in cozily, she was not sure that she would not wake up in the garret in the morning.

"And oh, Charles, dear," Mrs. Carmichael said to her husband, when she went downstairs to him, "we must get that lonely look out of her eyes! It isn't a child's look at all. I couldn't bear to see it in one of my own children. What the poor little love must have had to bear in that dreadful woman's house! But, surely, she will forget it in time."

But though the lonely look passed away from Sara's face, she never quite forgot the garret at Miss Minchin's; and, indeed, she always liked to remember the wonderful night when the tired princess crept upstairs, cold and wet, and opening the door found fairy-land waiting for her. And there was no one of the many stories she was always being called upon to tell in the nursery of the Large Family which was more popular than that particular one; and there was no one of whom the Large Family were so fond as of Sara. Mr. Carrisford did not die, but recovered, and Sara went to live with him; and no real princess could have been better taken care of than she was. It seemed that the Indian Gentleman could not do enough to make her happy, and to repay her for the past; and the Lascar was her devoted slave. As her odd little face grew brighter, it grew so pretty and interesting that Mr. Carrisford used to sit and watch it many an evening, as they sat by the fire together.

They became great friends, and they used to spend hours reading and talking together: and, in a very short time, there was no pleasanter sight to the Indian Gentleman than Sara sitting in her big chair on the opposite side of the hearth, with a book on her knee and her soft, dark hair tumbling over her warm cheeks. She had a pretty habit of looking up at him suddenly, with a bright smile, and then he would often say to her:

"Are you happy, Sara?"

And then she would answer:

"I feel like a real princess, Uncle Tom."

He had told her to call him Uncle Tom.

"There doesn't seem to be anything left to 'suppose,'" she added.

There was a little joke between them that he was a magician, and so could do anything he liked; and it was one of his pleasures to invent plans to surprise her with enjoyments she had not thought of. Scarcely a day passed in which he did not do something new for her. Sometimes she found new flowers in her room; sometimes a fanciful little gift tucked into some odd corner; sometimes a new book on her pillow;—once as they sat together in the evening they heard the scratch of a heavy paw on the door of the room, and when Sara went to find out what it was, there stood a great dog—a splendid Russian boar-hound with a grand silver and gold collar. Stooping to read the inscription upon the collar, Sara was delighted to read the words, "I am Boris; I serve the Princess Sara."

Then there was a sort of fairy nursery arranged for the entertainment of the juvenile members of the Large Family, who were always coming to see Sara and the Lascar and the monkey. Sara was as fond of the Large Family as they were of her. She soon felt as if she were a member of it, and the companionship of the healthy, happy children was very good for her. All the children rather looked up to her and regarded her as the cleverest and most brilliant of creatures—particularly after it was discovered that she not only knew stories of every kind, and could invent new ones at a moment's notice, but that she could help with lessons, and speak French and German, and discourse with the Lascar in Hindustani.

It was rather a painful experience for Miss Minchin watch her ex-pupil's fortunes, as she had the daily opportunity to do, and to feel that she had made a serious mistake, from a business point of view. She had even tried to retrieve it by suggesting that Sara's education should be continued under her care, and had gone to the length of making an appeal to the child herself.

"I have always been very fond of you," she said.

Then Sara fixed her eyes upon her and gave her one of her odd looks.

"Have you?" she answered.

"Yes," said Miss Minchin. "Amelia and I have always said you were the cleverest child we had with us, and I am sure we could make you happy—as a parlor boarder."

Sara thought of the garret and the day her ears were boxed,—and of that other day, that dreadful, desolate day when she had been told that she belonged to nobody; that she had no home and no friends,—and she kept her eyes fixed on Miss Minchin's face.

"You know why I would not stay with you," she said.

And it seems probable that Miss Minchin did, for after that simple answer she had not the boldness to pursue the subject. She merely sent in a bill for the expense of Sara's education and support, and she made it quite large enough. And because Mr. Carrisford thought Sara would wish it paid, it was paid. When Mr. Carmichael paid it he had a brief interview with Miss Minchin in which he expressed his opinion with much clearness and force; and it is quite certain that Miss Minchin did not enjoy the conversation.

Sara had been about a month with Mr. Carrisford, and had begun to realize that her happiness was not a dream, when one night the Indian Gentleman saw that she sat a long time with her cheek on her hand looking at the fire.

"What are you 'supposing,' Sara?" he asked. Sara looked up with a bright color on her cheeks.

"I *was* 'supposing,'" she said; "I was remembering that hungry day, and a child I saw."

"But there were a great many hungry days," said the

Indian Gentleman, with a rather sad tone in his voice. "Which hungry day was it?"

"I forgot you didn't know," said Sara. "It was the day I found the things in my garret."

And then she told him the story of the bun-shop, and the fourpence, and the child who was hungrier than herself; and somehow as she told it, though she told it very simply indeed, the Indian Gentleman found it necessary to shade his eyes with his hand and look down at the floor.

"And I was 'supposing' a kind of plan," said Sara, when she had finished; "I was thinking I would like to do something."

"What is it?" said her guardian in a low tone. "You may do anything you like to do, Princess."

"I was wondering," said Sara,—"you know you say I have a great deal of money—and I was wondering if I could go and see the bun-woman and tell her that if, when hungry children—particularly on those dreadful days— come and sit on the steps or look in at the window, she would just call them in and give them something to eat, she might send the bills to me and I would pay them— could I do that?"

"You shall do it to-morrow morning," said the Indian Gentleman.

"Thank you," said Sara; "you see I know what it is to be hungry, and it is very hard when one can't even *pretend* it away."

"Yes, yes, my dear," said the Indian Gentleman. "Yes, it must be. Try to forget it. Come and sit on this footstool near my knee, and only remember you are a princess."

"Yes," said Sara, "and I can give buns and bread to the Populace." And she went and sat on the stool, and the Indian Gentleman (he used to like her to call him that, too, sometimes,—in fact very often) drew her small, dark head down upon his knee and stroked her hair.

The next morning a carriage drew up before the door of the baker's shop, and a gentleman and a little girl got

out,—oddly enough, just as the bun-woman was putting a
tray of smoking hot buns into the window. When Sara
entered the shop the woman turned and looked at her
and, leaving the buns, came and stood behind the
counter. For a moment she looked at Sara very hard
indeed, and then her good-natured face lighted up.

"I'm that sure I remember you, miss," she said. "And
yet——"

"Yes," said Sara, "once you gave me six buns for
fourpence, and——"

"And you gave five of 'em to a beggar-child," said the
woman. "I've always remembered it. I couldn't make it out
at first. I beg pardon, sir, but there's not many young people that notices a hungry face in that way, and I've
thought of it many a time. Excuse the liberty, miss, but
you look rosier and better than you did that day."

"I am better, thank you," said Sara, "and—and I am happier, and I have come to ask you to do something for me."

"Me, miss!" exclaimed the woman, "why, bless you, yes,
miss! What can I do?"

And then Sara made her little proposal, and the woman
listened to it with an astonished face.

"Why, bless me!" she said, when she had heard it all.
"Yes, miss, it'll be a pleasure to me to do it. I am a working woman, myself, and can't afford to do much on my
own account, and there's sights of trouble on every side;
but if you'll excuse me, I'm bound to say I've given many
a bit of bread away since that wet afternoon, just along o'
thinkin' of you. An' how wet an' cold you was, an' how you
looked,—an' yet you give away your hot buns as if you
was a princess."

The Indian Gentleman smiled involuntarily, and Sara
smiled a little too. "She looked so hungry," she said. "She
was hungrier than I was."

"She was starving," said the woman. "Many's the time
she's told me of it since—how she sat there in the wet,
and felt as if a wolf was a-tearing at her poor young
insides."

"Oh, have you seen her since then?" exclaimed Sara. "Do you know where she is?"

"I know!" said the woman. "Why, she's in that there back room now, miss, an' has been for a month, an' a decent, well-meaning girl she's going to turn out, an' such a help to me in the day shop, an' in the kitchen, as you'd scarce believe, knowing how she's lived."

She stepped to the door of the little back parlor and spoke; and the next minute a girl came out and followed her behind the counter. And actually it was the beggar-child, clean and neatly clothed, and looking as if she had not been hungry for a long time. She looked shy, but she had a nice face, now that she was no longer a savage; and the wild look had gone from her eyes. And she knew Sara in an instant, and stood and looked at her as if she could never look enough.

"You see," said the woman, "I told her to come here when she was hungry, and when she'd come I'd give her odd jobs to do, an' I found she was willing, an' somehow I got to like her; an' the end of it was I've given her a place an' a home, an' she helps me, an' behaves as well, an' is as thankful as a girl can be. Her name's Anne—she has no other."

The two children stood and looked at each other a few moments. In Sara's eyes a new thought was growing.

"I'm glad you have such a good home," she said. "Perhaps Mrs. Brown will let you give the buns and bread to the children—perhaps you would like to do it—because you know what it is to be hungry, too."

"Yes, miss," said the girl.

And somehow Sara felt as if she understood her, though the girl said nothing more, and only stood still and looked, and looked after her as she went out of the shop and got into the carriage and drove away.

Little Saint Elizabeth

She had not been brought up in America at all. She had been born in France, in a beautiful *château,* and she had been born heiress to a great fortune, but, nevertheless, just now she felt as if she was very poor, indeed. And yet her home was in one of the most splendid houses in New York. She had a lovely suite of apartments of her own, though she was only eleven years old. She had had her own carriage and a saddle horse, a train of masters, and governesses, and servants, and was regarded by all the children of the neighborhood as a sort of grand and mysterious little princess, whose incomings and outgoings were to be watched with the greatest interest.

"There she is," they would cry, flying to their windows to look at her. "She is going out in her carriage." "She is dressed all in black velvet and splendid fur." "That is her own, own, carriage." "She has millions of money; and she can have anything she wants—Jane says so!" "She is very pretty, too; but she is so pale and has such big, sorrowful, black eyes. I should not be sorrowful if I were in her place; but Jane says the servants say she is always quiet and looks sad." "Her maid says she lived with her aunt, and her aunt made her too religious."

She rarely lifted her large dark eyes to look at them with any curiosity. She was not accustomed to the society of children. She had never had a child companion in her life, and these little Americans, who were so very rosy and gay, and who went out to walk or drive with groups of brothers

74

and sisters, and even ran in the street, laughing and playing and squabbling healthily—these children amazed her.

Poor little Saint Elizabeth! She had not lived a very natural or healthy life herself, and she knew absolutely nothing of real childish pleasures. You see, it had occurred in this way: When she was a baby of two years her young father and mother died, within a week of each other, of a terrible fever, and the only near relatives the little one had were her Aunt Clotilde and Uncle Bertrand. Her Aunt Clotilde lived in Normandy—her Uncle Bertrand in New York. As these two were her only guardians, and as Bertrand de Rochemont was a gay bachelor, fond of pleasure and knowing nothing of babies, it was natural that he should be very willing that his elder sister should undertake the rearing and education of the child.

"Only," he wrote to Mademoiselle de Rochemont, "don't end by training her for an abbess, my dear Clotilde."

There was a very great difference between these two people—the distance between the gray stone *château* in Normandy and the brown stone mansion in New York was not nearly so great as the distance and difference between the two lives. And yet it was said that in her first youth Mademoiselle de Rochemont had been as gay and fond of pleasure as either of her brothers. And then, when her life was at its brightest and gayest—when she was a beautiful and brilliant young woman—she had had a great and bitter sorrow, which had changed her for ever. From that time she had never left the house in which she had been born, and had lived the life of a nun in everything but being enclosed in convent walls. At first she had had her parents to take care of, but when they died she had been left entirely alone in the great *château,* and devoted herself to prayer and works of charity among the villagers and country people.

"Ah! she is good—she is a saint Mademoiselle," the poor people always said when speaking of her; but they also always looked a little awe-stricken when she appeared, and never were sorry when she left them.

She was a tall woman, with a pale, rigid, handsome face, which never smiled. She did nothing but good deeds, but however grateful her pensioners might be, nobody would ever have dared to dream of loving her. She was just and cold and severe. She wore always a straight black serge gown, broad bands of white linen, and a rosary and crucifix at her waist. She read nothing but religious works and legends of the saints and martyrs, and adjoining her private apartments was a little stone chapel, where the servants said she used to kneel on the cold floor before the altar and pray for hours in the middle of the night.

The little *curé* of the village, who was plump and comfortable, and who had the kindest heart and the most cheerful soul in the world, used to remonstrate with her, always in a roundabout way, however, never quite as if he were referring directly to herself.

"One must not let one's self become the stone image of goodness," he said once. "Since one is really of flesh and blood, and lives among flesh and blood, that is not best. No, no; it is not best."

But Mademoiselle de Rochemont never seemed exactly of flesh and blood—she was more like a marble female saint who had descended from her pedestal to walk upon the earth.

And she did not change, even when the baby Elizabeth was brought to her. She attended strictly to the child's comfort and prayed many prayers for her innocent soul, but it can be scarcely said that her manner was any softer or that she smiled more. At first Elizabeth used to scream at the sight of the black, nun-like dress and the rigid, handsome face, but in course of time she became accustomed to them, and, through living in an atmosphere so silent and without brightness, a few months changed her from a laughing, romping baby into a pale, quiet child, who rarely made any childish noise at all.

In this quiet way she became fond of her aunt. She saw little of anyone but the servants, who were all trained to quietness also. As soon as she was old enough her aunt began her religious training. Before she could speak plainly she heard legends of saints and stories of martyrs. She was taken into the little chapel and taught to pray there. She believed in miracles, and would not have been surprised at any moment if she had met the Child Jesus or the Virgin in the beautiful rambling gardens which surrounded the *château*. She was a sensitive, imaginative child, and the sacred romances she heard filled all her mind and made up her little life. She wished to be a saint herself, and spent hours in wandering in the terraced rose gardens wondering if such a thing was possible in modern days, and what she must do to obtain such holy victory. Her chief sorrow was that she knew herself to be delicate and very timid—so timid that she often suffered when people did not suspect it—and she was afraid that she was not brave enough to be a martyr. Once, poor little one! when she was alone in her room, she held her hand over a burning wax candle, but the pain was so terrible that she could not keep it there. Indeed, she fell back white and faint, and sank upon her chair, breathless and in tears, because she felt sure that she could not chant holy songs if she were being burned at the stake. She had been vowed to the Virgin in her babyhood, and was always dressed in white and blue, but her little dress was a small conventual robe, straight and narrow cut, of white woollen stuff, and banded plainly with blue at the waist. She did not look like other children, but she was very sweet and gentle, and her pure little pale face and large, dark eyes had a lovely dreamy look. When she was old enough to visit the poor with her Aunt Clotilde—and she was hardly seven years old when it was considered proper that she should begin—the villagers did not stand in awe of her. They began to adore her, almost to worship her, as if she had, indeed, been a sacred child. The little ones delighted to look at her, to draw near her sometimes and touch her soft white and blue robe. And, when they did so, she always returned their looks with such a tender, sympathetic smile, and spoke to them in so gentle a voice, that they were in ecstasies. They used to talk her over, tell stories about her when they were playing together afterwards.

"The little Mademoiselle," they said, "she is a child saint. I have heard them say so. Sometimes there is a little light round her head. One day her little white robe will begin to shine too, and her long sleeves will be wings, and she will spread them and ascend through the blue sky to Paradise. You will see if it is not so."

So, in this secluded world in the gray old *château,* with no companion but her aunt, with no occupation but her studies and her charities, with no thoughts but those of saints and religious exercises, Elizabeth lived until she was eleven years old. Then a great grief befell her. One morning, Mademoiselle de Rochemont did not leave her room at the regular hour. As she never broke a rule she had made for herself and her household, this occasioned great wonder. Her old maid servant waited half an hour— went to her door, and took the liberty of listening to hear if she was up and moving about her room. There was no sound. Old Alice returned, looking quite agitated. "Would Mademoiselle Elizabeth mind entering to see if all was well? Mademoiselle her aunt might be in the chapel."

Elizabeth went. Her aunt was not in her room. Then she must be in the chapel. The child entered the sacred little place. The morning sun was streaming in through the stained-glass windows above the altar—a broad ray of mingled brilliant colors slanted to the stone floor and warmly touched a dark figure lying there. It was Aunt Clotilde, who had sunk forward while kneeling at prayer and had died in the night.

That was what the doctors said when they were sent for. She had been dead some hours—she had died of disease of the heart, and apparently without any pain or knowledge of the change coming to her. Her face was serene and beautiful, and the rigid look had melted away. Someone said she looked like little Mademoiselle Elizabeth; and her old servant Alice wept very much, and said, "Yes—yes—it was so when she was young, before her unhappiness came. She had the same beautiful little face, but she was more gay, more of the world. Yes, they were much alike then."

Less than two months from that time Elizabeth was living in the home of her Uncle Bertrand, in New York. He had come to Normandy for her himself, and taken her back with him across the Atlantic. She was richer than ever now, as a great deal of her Aunt Clotilde's money had been left to her, and Uncle Bertrand was her guardian. He was a handsome, elegant, clever man, who, having lived long in America and being fond of American life, did not appear very much like a Frenchman—at least he did not appear so to Elizabeth, who had only seen the *curé* and the doctor of the village. Secretly he was very much embarrassed at the prospect of taking care of a little girl, but family pride, and the fact that such a very little girl, who was also such a very great heiress, *must* be taken care of sustained him. But when he first saw Elizabeth he could not restrain an exclamation of consternation.

She entered the room, when she was sent for, clad in a strange little nun-like robe of black serge, made as like her dead aunt's as possible. At her small waist were the rosary and crucifix, and in her hand she held a missal she had forgotten in her agitation to lay down——

"But, my dear child," exclaimed Uncle Bertrand, staring at her aghast.

He managed to recover himself very quickly, and was, in his way, very kind to her; but the first thing he did was to send to Paris for a fashionable maid and fashionable mourning.

"Because, as you will see," he remarked to Alice, "we cannot travel as we are. It is a costume for a convent or the stage."

Before she took off her little conventual robe, Elizabeth went to the village to visit all her poor. The *curé* went with her and shed tears himself when the people wept and kissed her little hand. When the child returned, she went into the chapel and remained there for a long time.

She felt as if she was living in a dream when all the old life was left behind and she found herself in the big luxurious house in the gay New York street. Nothing that could be done for her comfort had been left undone. She had several beautiful rooms, a wonderful governess, different masters to teach her, her own retinue of servants as, indeed, has been already said.

But, secretly, she felt bewildered and almost terrified, everything was so new, so strange, so noisy, and so brilliant. The dress she wore made her feel unlike herself; the books they gave her were full of pictures and stories of worldly things of which she knew nothing. Her carriage was brought to the door and she went out with her governess, driving round and round the park with scores of other people who looked at her curiously, she did not know why. The truth was that her refined little face was very beautiful indeed, and her soft dark eyes still wore the dreamy spiritual look which made her unlike the rest of the world.

"She looks like a little princess," she heard her uncle say one day. "She will be some day a beautiful, an enchanting woman—her mother was so when she died at twenty, but she had been brought up differently. This one is a little devotee. I am afraid of her. Her governess tells me she rises in the night to pray." He said it with light laughter to some of his gay friends by whom he had wished the child to be seen. He did not know that his gayety filled her with fear and pain. She had been taught to believe gayety worldly and sinful, and his whole life was filled with it. He had brilliant parties—he did not go to church—he had no pensioners—he seemed to think of nothing but pleasure. Poor little Saint Elizabeth prayed for his soul many an hour when he was asleep after a grand dinner or supper party.

He could not possibly have dreamed that there was no one of whom she stood in such dread; her timidity increased tenfold in his presence. When he sent for her and she went into the library to find him luxurious in his arm chair, a novel on his knee, a cigar in his white hand, a tolerant, half cynical smile on his handsome mouth, she could scarcely answer his questions, and could never find courage to tell what she so earnestly desired. She had found out early that Aunt Clotilde and the *curé,* and the life they had led, had only aroused in his mind a half-pitying amusement. It seemed to her that he did not understand and had strange sacrilegious thoughts about them—he did not believe in miracles—he smiled when she spoke of saints. How could she tell him that she wished to spend all her money in building churches and giving alms to the poor? That was what she wished to tell him—that she wanted money to send back to the village, that she wanted to give it to the poor people she saw in the streets, to those who lived in the miserable places.

But when she found herself face to face with him and he said some witty thing to her and seemed to find her only amusing, all her courage failed her. Sometimes she thought she would throw herself upon her knees before him and beg him to send her back to Normandy—to let her live alone in the *château* as her Aunt Clotilde had done.

One morning she arose very early, and knelt a long time before the little altar she had made for herself in her dressing room. It was only a table with some black velvet thrown over it, a crucifix, a saintly image, and some flowers standing upon it. She had put on, when she got up, the quaint black serge robe, because she felt more at home in it, and her heart was full of determination. The night before she had received a letter from the *curé* and it had contained sad news. A fever had broken out in her beloved village, the vines had done badly, there was sickness among the cattle, there was already beginning to be suffering, and if something were not done for the people they would not know how to face the winter. In the time of Mademoiselle de Rochemont they had always been made comfortable and happy at Christmas. What was to be done? The *curé* ventured to write to Mademoiselle Elizabeth.

The poor child had scarcely slept at all. Her dear village! Her dear people! The children would be hungry; the cows would die; there would be no fires to warm those who were old.

"I must go to uncle," she said, pale and trembling. "I must ask him to give me money. I am afraid, but it is right to mortify the spirit. The martyrs went to the stake. The holy Saint Elizabeth was ready to endure anything that she might do her duty and help the poor."

Because she had been called Elizabeth she had thought and read a great deal of the saint whose namesake she was—the saintly Elizabeth whose husband was so wicked and cruel, and who wished to prevent her from doing good deeds. And oftenest of all she had read the legend which told that one day as Elizabeth went out with a basket of food to give to the poor and hungry, she had met her savage husband, who had demanded that she should tell him what she was carrying, and when she replied, "Roses," and he tore the cover from the basket to see if she spoke the truth, a miracle had been performed, and the basket was filled with roses, so that she had been saved from her husband's cruelty, and also from telling an untruth. To little Elizabeth this legend had been beautiful and quite real—it proved that if one were doing good, the saints would take care of one. Since she had been in her new home, she had, half consciously, compared her Uncle Bertrand with the wicked Landgrave, though she was too gentle and just to think he was really cruel, as Saint Elizabeth's husband had been, only he did not care for the poor, and loved only the world—and surely that was wicked. She had been taught that to care for the world at all was a fatal sin.

She did not eat any breakfast. She thought she would fast until she had done what she intended to do. It had been her Aunt Clotilde's habit to fast very often.

She waited anxiously to hear that her Uncle Bertrand had left his room. He always rose late, and this morning he was later than usual as he had had a long gay dinner party the night before.

It was nearly twelve before she heard his door open. Then she went quickly to the staircase. Her heart was beating so fast that she put her little hand to her side and waited a moment to regain her breath. She felt quite cold.

"Perhaps I must wait until he has eaten his breakfast," she said. "Perhaps I must not disturb him yet. It would make him displeased. I will wait—yes, for a little while."

She did not return to her room, but waited upon the stairs. It seemed to be a long time. It appeared that a friend breakfasted with him. She heard a gentleman come in and recognized his voice, which she had heard before. She did not know what the gentleman's name was, but she had met him going in and out with her uncle once or twice, and had thought he had a kind face and kind eyes. He had looked at her in an interested way when he spoke to her—even as if he were a little curious, and she had wondered why he did so.

When the door of the breakfast room opened and shut as the servants went in, she could hear the two laughing and talking. They seemed to be enjoying themselves very much. Once she heard an order given for the mail phaeton. They were evidently going out as soon as the meal was over.

At last the door opened and they were coming out. Elizabeth ran down the stairs and stood in a small reception room. Her heart began to beat faster than ever.

"The blessed martyrs were not afraid," she whispered to herself.

"Uncle Bertrand!" she said, as he approached, and she scarcely knew her own faint voice. "Uncle Bertrand——"

He turned, and seeing her, started, and exclaimed, rather impatiently—evidently he was at once amazed and displeased to see her. He was in a hurry to get out, and the sight of her odd little figure, standing in its straight black robe between the *portières,* the slender hands clasped on the breast, the small pale face and great dark eyes uplifted, was certainly a surprise to him.

"Elizabeth!" he said, "what do you wish? Why do you come downstairs? And that impossible dress! Why do you wear it again? It is not suitable."

"Uncle Bertrand," said the child, clasping her hands still more tightly, her eyes growing larger in her excitement and terror under his displeasure, "it is that I want money—a great deal. I beg your pardon if I derange you. It is for the poor. Moreover, the *curé* has written the people of the village are ill—the vineyards did not yield well. They must have money. I must send them some."

Uncle Bertrand shrugged his shoulders.

"That is the message of *monsieur le curé,* is it?" he said. "He wants money! My dear Elizabeth, I must inquire further. You have a fortune, but I cannot permit you to throw it away. You are a child, and do not understand——"

"But," cried Elizabeth, trembling with agitation, "they are so poor when one does not help them: their vineyards are so little, and if the year is bad they must starve. Aunt Clotilde gave to them every year—even in the good years. She said they must be cared for like children."

"That was your Aunt Clotilde's charity," replied her uncle. "Sometimes she was not so wise as she was devout. I must know more of this. I have no time at present. I am going out of town. In a few days I will reflect upon it. Tell your maid to give that hideous garment away. Go out to drive—amuse yourself—you are too pale."

Elizabeth looked at his handsome, careless face in utter helplessness. This was a matter of life and death to her; to him it meant nothing.

"But it is winter," she panted, breathlessly; "there is snow. Soon it will be Christmas, and they will have nothing—no candles for the church, no little manger for the holy child, nothing for the poorest ones. And the children——"

"It shall be thought of later," said Uncle Bertrand. "I am too busy now. Be reasonable, my child, and run away. You detain me."

He left her with a slight impatient shrug of his shoulders and the slight amused smile on his lips. She heard him speak to his friend.

"She was brought up by one who had renounced the world," he said, "and she has already renounced it herself—*pauvre petite enfant!* At eleven years she wishes to devote her fortune to the poor and herself to the Church."

Elizabeth sank back into the shadow of the *portières*. Great burning tears filled her eyes and slipped down her cheeks, falling upon her breast.

"He does not care," she said; "he does not know. And I do no one good—no one." And she covered her face with her hands and stood sobbing all alone.

When she returned to her room she was so pale that her maid looked at her anxiously, and spoke of it afterwards to the other servants. They were all fond of Mademoiselle Elizabeth. She was always kind and gentle to everybody.

Nearly all the day she sat, poor little saint! by her window looking out at the passers-by in the snowy street. But she scarcely saw the people at all, her thoughts were far away, in the little village where she had always spent her Christmas before. Her Aunt Clotilde had allowed her at such times to do so much. There had not been a house she had not carried some gift to; not a child who had been forgotten. And the church on Christmas morning had been so beautiful with flowers from the hot-houses of the *château*. It was for the church, indeed, that the conservatories were chiefly kept up. Mademoiselle de Rochemont would scarcely have permitted herself such luxuries.

But there would not be flowers this year, the *château* was closed; there were no longer gardeners at work, the church would be bare and cold, the people would have no gifts, there would be no pleasure in the little peasants' faces. Little Saint Elizabeth wrung her slight hands together in her lap.

"Oh," she cried, "what can I do? And then there is the poor here—so many. And I do nothing. The Saints will be angry; they will not intercede for me. I shall be lost!"

It was not alone the poor she had left in her village who were a grief to her. As she drove through the streets she saw now and then haggard faces; and when she had questioned a servant who had one day come to her to ask for charity for a poor child at the door, she had found that in parts of this great, bright city which she had not seen, there was said to be cruel want and suffering, as in all great cities.

"And it is so cold now," she thought, "with the snow on the ground."

The lamps in the street were just beginning to be lighted when her Uncle Bertrand returned. It appeared that he had brought back with him the gentleman with the kind face. They were to dine together, and Uncle Bertrand desired that Mademoiselle Elizabeth should join them. Evidently the journey out of town had been delayed for a day at least. There came also another message: Monsieur de Rochemont wished Mademoiselle to send to him by her maid a certain box of antique ornaments which had been given to her by her Aunt Clotilde. Elizabeth had known less of the value of these jewels than of their beauty. She knew they were beautiful, and that they had belonged to her Aunt Clotilde in the gay days of her triumphs as a beauty and a brilliant and adored young woman, but it seemed that they were also very curious, and Monsieur de Rochemont wished his friend to see them. When Elizabeth went downstairs she found them examining them together.

"They must be put somewhere for safe keeping," Uncle Bertrand was saying. "It should have been done before. I will attend to it."

The gentleman with the kind eyes looked at Elizabeth with an interested expression as she came into the room. Her slender little figure in its black velvet dress, her delicate little face with its large soft sad eyes, the gentle gravity of her manner made her seem quite unlike other children.

He did not seem simply to find her amusing, as her

Uncle Bertrand did. She was always conscious that behind Uncle Bertrand's most serious expression there was lurking a faint smile as he watched her, but this visitor looked at her in a different way. He was a doctor, she discovered. Dr. Norris, her uncle called him, and Elizabeth wondered if perhaps his profession had not made him quick of sight and kind.

She felt that it must be so when she heard him talk at dinner. She found that he did a great deal of work among the very poor—that he had a hospital, where he received little children who were ill—who had perhaps met with accidents, and could not be taken care of in their wretched homes. He spoke most frequently of terrible quarters, which he called Five Points; the greatest poverty and suffering was there. And he spoke of it with such eloquent sympathy, that even Uncle Bertrand began to listen with interest.

"Come," he said, "you are a rich, idle fellow, De Rochemont, and we want rich, idle fellows to come and look into all this and do something for us. You must let me take you with me some day."

"It would disturb me too much, my good Norris," said Uncle Bertrand, with a slight shudder. "I should not enjoy my dinner after it."

"Then go without your dinner," said Dr. Norris. "These people do. You have too many dinners. Give up one."

Uncle Bertrand shrugged his shoulders and smiled.

"It is Elizabeth who fasts," he said. "Myself, I prefer to dine. And yet, some day, I may have the fancy to visit this place with you."

Elizabeth could scarcely have been said to dine this evening. She could not eat. She sat with her large, sad eyes fixed upon Dr. Norris' face as he talked. Every word he uttered sank deep into her heart. The want and suffering of which he spoke were more terrible than anything she had ever heard of—it had been nothing like this in the village. Oh! no, no. As she thought of it there was such a look in her dark eyes as almost startled Dr. Norris several times when he glanced at her, but as he did not know the particulars of her life with her aunt and the strange training she had had, he could not possibly have guessed what was going on in her mind, and how much effect his stories were having. The beautiful little face touched him very much, and the pretty French accent with which the child spoke seemed very musical to him, and added a great charm to the gentle, serious answers she made to the remarks he addressed to her. He could not help seeing that something had made little Mademoiselle Elizabeth a pathetic and singular little creature, and he continually wondered what it was.

"Do you think she is a happy child?" he asked Monsieur de Rochemont when they were alone together over their cigars and wine.

"Happy?" said Uncle Bertrand, with his light smile. "She has been taught, my friend, that to be happy upon earth is a crime. That was my good sister's creed. One must devote one's self, not to happiness, but entirely to good works. I think I have told you that she, this little one, desires to give all her fortune to the poor. Having heard you this evening, she will wish to bestow it upon your Five Points."

When, having retired from the room with a grave and stately little obeisance to her uncle and his guest, Elizabeth had gone upstairs, it had not been with the intention of going to bed. She sent her maid away and knelt before her altar for a long time.

"The Saints will tell me what to do," she said. "The good Saints, who are always gracious, they will vouchsafe to me some thought which will instruct me if I remain long enough at prayer."

She remained in prayer a long time. When at last she arose from her knees it was long past midnight, and she was tired and weak, but the thought had not been given to her.

But just as she laid her head upon her pillow it came. The ornaments given to her by her Aunt Clotilde somebody would buy them. They were her own—it would be right to sell them—to what better use could they be put? Was it not what Aunt Clotilde would have desired? Had she not told her stories of the good and charitable who had sold the clothes from their bodies that the miserable might be helped? Yes, it was right. These things must be done. All else was vain and useless and of the world. But it would require courage—great courage. To go out alone to find a place where the people would buy the jewels—perhaps there might be some who would not want them. And then when they were sold to find this poor and unhappy quarter of which her uncle's guest had spoken, and to give to those who needed—all by herself. Ah! what courage it would require. And then Uncle Bertrand, some day he would ask about the ornaments, and discover all, and his anger might be terrible. No one had ever been angry with her; how could she bear it. But had not the Saints and Martyrs borne everything? had they not gone to the stake and the rack with smiles? She thought of Saint Elizabeth and the cruel Landgrave. It could not be even so bad as that—but whatever the result was it must be borne.

So at last she slept, and there was upon her gentle little face so sweetly sad a look that when her maid came to waken her in the morning she stood by the bedside for some moments looking down upon her pityingly.

The day seemed very long and sorrowful to the poor child. It was full of anxious thoughts and plannings. She was so innocent and inexperienced, so ignorant of all practical things. She had decided that it would be best to wait until evening before going out, and then to take the jewels and try to sell them to some jeweller. She did not understand the difficulties that would lie in her way, but she felt very timid.

Her maid had asked permission to go out for the evening and Monsieur de Rochemont was to dine out, so that she found it possible to leave the house without attracting attention.

As soon as the streets were lighted she took the case of

ornaments, and going downstairs very quietly, let herself out. The servants were dining, and she was seen by none of them.

When she found herself in the snowy street she felt strangely bewildered. She had never been out unattended before, and she knew nothing of the great busy city. When she turned into the more crowded thoroughfares, she saw several times that the passers-by glanced at her curiously. Her timid look, her foreign air and richly furred dress, and the fact that she was a child and alone at such an hour, could not fail to attract attention; but though she felt confused and troubled she went bravely on. It was some time before she found a jeweller's shop, and when she entered it the men behind the counter looked at her in amazement. But she went to the one nearest to her and laid the case of jewels on the counter before him.

"I wish," she said, in her soft low voice, and with the pretty accent, "I wish that you should buy these."

The man stared at her, and at the ornaments, and then at her again.

"I beg pardon, miss," he said.

Elizabeth repeated her request.

"I will speak to Mr. Moetyler," he said, after a moment of hesitation.

He went to the other end of the shop to an elderly man who sat behind a desk. After he had spoken a few words, the elderly man looked up as if surprised; then he glanced at Elizabeth; then, after speaking a few more words, he came forward.

"You wish to sell these?" he said, looking at the case of jewels with a puzzled expression.

"Yes," Elizabeth answered.

He bent over the case and took up one ornament after the other and examined them closely. After he had done this he looked at the little girl's innocent, trustful face, seeming more puzzled than before.

"Are they your own?" he inquired.

"Yes, they are mine," she replied, timidly.

"Do you know how much they are worth?"

"I know that they are worth much money," said Elizabeth. "I have heard it said so."

"Do your friends know that you are going to sell them?"

"No," Elizabeth said, a faint color rising in her delicate face. "But it is right that I should do it."

The man spent a few moments in examining them again and, having done so, spoke hesitatingly.

"I am afraid we cannot buy them," he said. "It would be impossible, unless your friends first gave their permission."

"Impossible!" said Elizabeth, and tears rose in her eyes, making them look softer and more wistful than ever.

"We could not do it," said the jeweller. "It is out of the question under the circumstances."

"Do you think," faltered the poor little saint, "do you think that nobody will buy them?"

"I am afraid not," was the reply. "No respectable firm who would pay their real value. If you'll take my advice, young lady, you will take them home and consult your friends."

He spoke kindly, but Elizabeth was overwhelmed with disappointment. She did not know enough of the world to understand that a richly dressed little girl who offered valuable jewels for sale at night must be a strange and unusual sight.

When she found herself on the street again, her long lashes were heavy with tears.

"If no one will buy them," she said, "what shall I do?"

She walked a long way—so long that she was very tired—and offered them at several places, but as she chanced to enter only respectable shops, the same thing happened each time. She was looked at curiously and questioned, but no one would buy.

"They are mine," she would say. "It is right that I should sell them." But everyone stared and seemed puzzled, and in the end refused.

At last, after much wandering, she found herself in a

poorer quarter of the city; the streets were narrower and
dirtier, and the people began to look squalid and
wretchedly dressed; there were smaller shops and dingy
houses. She saw unkempt men and women and uncared
for little children. The poverty of the poor she had seen in
her own village seemed comfort and luxury by contrast.
She had never dreamed of anything like this. Now and
then she felt faint with pain and horror. But she went on.

"They have no vineyards," she said to herself. "No trees
and flowers—it is all dreadful—there is nothing. They
need help more than the others. To let them suffer so, and
not to give them charity, would be a great crime."

She was so full of grief and excitement that she had
ceased to notice how everyone looked at her—she saw
only the wretchedness, and dirt and misery. She did not
know, poor child! that she was surrounded by danger—
that she was not only in the midst of misery, but of dis-
honesty and crime. She had even forgotten her timidity—
that it was growing late, and that she was far from home,
and would not know how to return—she did not realize
that she had walked so far that she was almost exhausted
with fatigue.

She had brought with her all the money she possessed.
If she could not sell the jewels she could, at least, give
something to someone in want. But she did not know
to whom she must give first. When she had lived with
her Aunt Clotilde it had been their habit to visit the peasants in their houses. Must she enter one of these
houses—these dreadful places with the dark passages,
from which she heard many times riotous voices, and
even cries, issuing?

"But those who do good must feel no fear," she thought.
"It is only to have courage." At length something happened which caused her to pause before one of those
places. She heard sounds of pitiful moans and sobbing
from something crouched upon the broken steps. It
seemed like a heap of rags, but as she drew near she saw
by the light of the street lamp opposite that it was a

woman with her head in her knees, and a wretched child on each side of her. The children were shivering with cold and making low cries as if they were frightened.

Elizabeth stopped and then ascended the steps.

"Why is it that you cry?" she asked gently. "Tell me."

The woman did not answer at first, but when Elizabeth spoke again she lifted her head, and as soon as she saw the slender figure in its velvet and furs, and the pale, refined little face, she gave a great start.

"Lord have mercy on yez!" she said in a hoarse voice which sounded almost terrified. "Who are yez, an' what bees ye dow' in a place the loike o' this?"

"I came," said Elizabeth, "to see those who are poor. I wish to help them. I have great sorrow for them. It is right that the rich should help those who want. Tell me why you cry, and why your little children sit in the cold." Everybody had shown surprise to whom Elizabeth had spoken to-night, but no one had stared as this woman did.

"It's no place for the loike o' yez," she said. "An' it black noight, an' men and women wild in the drink; an' Pat Harrigan insoide bloind an' mad in liquor, an' it's turned me an' the children out he has to shlape in the snow—an' not the furst toime either. An' it's starvin' we are—starvin' an' no other," and she dropped her wretched head on her knees and began to moan again, and the children joined her.

"Don't let yez daddy hear yez," she said to them. "Whisht now—it's come out an' kill yez he will."

Elizabeth began to feel tremulous and faint.

"Is it that they have hunger?" she asked.

"Not a bite or sup have they had this day, nor yester-day," was the answer. "The good Saints have pity on us."

"Yes," said Elizabeth, "the good Saints have always pity. I will go and get some food—poor little ones."

She had seen a shop only a few yards away—she remembered passing it. Before the woman could speak again she was gone.

"Yes," she said, "I was sent to them—it is the answer to my prayer—it was not in vain that I asked so long."

When she entered the shop the few people who were in it stopped what they were doing to stare at her as others had done—but she scarcely saw that it was so.

"Give to me a basket," she said to the owner of the place. "Put in it some bread and wine—some of the things which are ready to eat. It is for a poor woman and her little ones who starve."

There was in the shop among others a red-faced woman with a cunning look in her eyes. She sidled out of the place and was waiting for Elizabeth when she came out.

"I'm starvin' too, little lady," she said. "There's many of us that way, an' it's not often them with money care about it. Give me something too," in a wheedling voice.

Elizabeth looked up at her, her pure ignorant eyes full of pity.

"I have great sorrows for you," she said. "Perhaps the poor woman will share her food with you."

"It's the money I need," said the woman.

"I have none left," answered Elizabeth. "I will come again."

"It's now I want it," the woman persisted. Then she looked covetously at Elizabeth's velvet fur-lined and trimmed cloak. "That's a pretty cloak you've on," she said. "You've got another, I daresay."

Suddenly she gave the cloak a pull, but the fastening did not give way as she had thought it would.

"Is it because you are cold that you want it?" said Elizabeth, in her gentle, innocent way. "I will give it to you. Take it."

Had not the holy ones in the legends given their garments to the poor? Why should she not give her cloak?

In an instant it was unclasped and snatched away, and the woman was gone. She did not even stay long enough to give thanks for the gift, and something in her haste and roughness made Elizabeth wonder and gave her a moment of tremor.

She made her way back to the place where the other woman and her children had been sitting; the cold wind made her shiver, and the basket was very heavy for her slender arm. Her strength seemed to be giving way.

As she turned the corner, a great, fierce gust of wind swept round it, and caught her breath and made her stagger. She thought she was going to fall; indeed, she would have fallen but that one of the tall men who were passing put out his arm and caught her. He was a well dressed man, in a heavy overcoat; he had gloves on. Elizabeth spoke in a faint tone.

"I thank you," she began, when the second man uttered a wild exclamation and sprang forward.

"Elizabeth!" he said, "Elizabeth!"

Elizabeth looked up and uttered a cry herself. It was her Uncle Bertrand who stood before her, and his companion, who had saved her from falling, was Dr. Norris.

For a moment it seemed as if they were almost struck dumb with horror; and then her Uncle Bertrand seized her by the arm in such agitation that he scarcely seemed himself—not the light, satirical, jesting Uncle Bertrand she had known at all.

"What does it mean?" he cried. "What are you doing here, in this horrible place alone? Do you know where it is you have come? What have you in your basket? Explain! explain!"

The moment of trial had come, and it seemed even more terrible than the poor child had imagined. The long strain and exertion had been too much for her delicate body. She felt that she could bear no more; the cold seemed to have struck to her very heart. She looked up at Monsieur de Rochemont's pale, excited face, and trembled from head to foot. A strange thought flashed into her mind. Saint Elizabeth, of Thuringia—the cruel Landgrave. Perhaps the Saints would help her too, since she was trying to do their bidding. Surely, surely it must be so!

"Speak!" repeated Monsieur de Rochemont. "Why is this? The basket—what have you in it?"

"Roses," said Elizabeth, "Roses." And then her strength deserted her—she fell upon her knees in the snow—the basket slipped from her arm, and the first thing which fell from it was—no, not roses,—there had been no miracle wrought—not roses, but the case of jewels which she had laid on the top of the other things that it might be the more easily carried.

"Roses!" cried Uncle Bertrand. "Is it that the child is mad? They are the jewels of my sister Clotilde."

Elizabeth clasped her hands and leaned towards Dr. Norris, the tears streaming from her uplifted eyes.

"Ah! monsieur," she sobbed, "you will understand. It was for the poor—they suffer so much. If we do not help them our souls will be lost. I did not mean to speak falsely. I thought the Saints—the Saints——" But her sobs filled her throat, and she could not finish. Dr. Norris stopped, and took her in his strong arms as if she had been a baby.

"Quick!" he said, imperatively; "we must return to the carriage, De Rochemont. This is a serious matter."

Elizabeth clung to him with trembling hands.

"But the poor woman who starves?" she cried. "The little children—they sit up on the step quite near—the food was for them! I pray you give it to them."

"Yes, they shall have it," said the Doctor. "Take the basket, De Rochemont—only a few doors below." And it appeared that there was something in his voice which seemed to render obedience necessary, for Monsieur de Rochemont actually did as he was told.

For a moment Dr. Norris put Elizabeth on her feet again, but it was only while he removed his overcoat and wrapped it about her slight shivering body.

"You are chilled through, poor child," he said; "and you are not strong enough to walk just now. You must let me carry you."

It was true that a sudden faintness had come upon her, and she could not restrain the shudder which shook her. It still shook her when she was placed in the carriage which the two gentlemen had thought it wiser to leave in one of the more respectable streets when they went to explore the worse ones together.

"What might not have occurred if we had not arrived at that instant!" said Uncle Bertrand when he got into the carriage. "As it is who knows what illness——"

"It will be better to say as little as possible now," said Dr. Norris.

"It was for the poor," said Elizabeth, trembling. "I had prayed to the Saints to tell me what was best. I thought I must go. I did not mean to do wrong. It was for the poor."

And while her Uncle Bertrand regarded her with a strangely agitated look, and Dr. Norris held her hand between his strong and warm ones, the tears rolled down her pure, pale little face.

She did not know until some time after what danger she had been in, that the part of the city into which she had wandered was the lowest and worst, and was in some quarters the home of thieves and criminals of every class. As her Uncle Bertrand has said, it was impossible to say what terrible thing might have happened if they had not met her so soon. It was Dr. Norris who explained it all to her as gently and kindly as was possible. She had always been fragile, and she had caught a severe cold which caused her an illness of some weeks. It was Dr. Norris who took care of her, and it was not long before her timidity was forgotten in her tender and trusting affection for him. She learned to watch for his coming, and to feel that she was no longer lonely. It was through him that her uncle permitted her to send to the *curé* a sum of money large enough to do all that was necessary. It was through him that the poor woman and her children were clothed and fed and protected. When she was well enough, he had promised that she should help him among his own poor. And through him—though she lost none of her sweet sympathy for those who suffered—she learned to live a more natural and child-like life, and to find that there were innocent, natural pleasures to be enjoyed in the world. In time she even ceased to be afraid of her Uncle Bertrand,

and to be quite happy in the great beautiful house. And as for Uncle Bertrand himself, he became very fond of her, and sometimes even helped her to dispense her charities. He had a light, gay nature, but he was kind at heart, and always disliked to see or think of suffering. Now and then he would give more lavishly than wisely, and then he would say, with his habitual graceful shrug of the shoulders—

"Yes, it appears I am not discreet. Finally, I think I must leave my charities to you, my good Norris—to you and Little Saint Elizabeth."

The Story of Prince Fairyfoot

Part I

Once upon a time, in the days of the fairies, there was in the far west country a kingdom which was called by the name of Stumpinghame. It was rather a curious country in several ways. In the first place, the people who lived there thought that Stumpinghame was all the world; they thought there was no world at all outside Stumpinghame. And they thought that the people of Stumpinghame knew everything that could possibly be known, and that what they did not know was of no consequence at all.

One idea common in Stumpinghame was really very unusual indeed. It was a peculiar taste in the matter of feet. In Stumpinghame, the larger a person's feet were, the more beautiful and elegant he or she was considered; and the more aristocratic and nobly born a man was, the more immense were his feet. Only the very lowest and most vulgar persons were ever known to have small feet. The King's feet were simply huge; so were the Queen's; so were those of the young princes and princesses. It had never occurred to anyone that a member of such a royal family could possibly disgrace himself by being born with small feet. Well, you may imagine, then, what a terrible and humiliating state of affairs arose when there was born into that royal family a little son, a prince, whose feet were so very small and slender and delicate that they would have been considered small even in other places than Stumpinghame. Grief and confusion seized the entire nation. The Queen fainted six times a day; the King had black rosettes fastened upon his crown; all the flags were at half-mast; and the court went into the deepest mourning. There had been born to Stumpinghame a royal prince with small feet, and nobody knew how the country could survive it!

Yet the disgraceful little prince survived it, and did not seem to mind at all. He was the prettiest and best tempered baby the royal nurse had ever seen. But for his small feet, he would have been the flower of the family. The royal nurse said to herself, and privately told his little royal highness's chief bottle-washer that she "never see a hinfant as took notice so, and sneezed as hintelligent." But, of course, the King and Queen could see nothing but his little feet, and very soon they made up their minds to send him away. So one day they had him bundled up and carried where they thought he might be quite forgotten. They sent him to the hut of a swineherd who lived deep, deep in a great forest which seemed to end nowhere.

They gave the swineherd some money, and some clothes for Fairyfoot, and told him, that if he would take care of the child, they would send money and clothes every year. As for themselves, they only wished to be sure of never seeing Fairyfoot again.

This pleased the swineherd well enough. He was poor, and he had a wife and ten children, and hundreds of swine to take care of, and he knew he could use the little Prince's money and clothes for his own family, and no one would find it out. So he let his wife take the little fellow, and as soon as the King's messengers had gone, the woman took the royal clothes off the Prince and put on him a coarse little nightgown, and gave all this things to her own children. But the baby Prince did not seem to mind that—he did not seem to mind anything, even though he had no name but Prince Fairyfoot, which had been given to him in contempt by the disgusted courtiers. He grew prettier and prettier every day, and long before the time when other children begin to walk, he could run about on his fairy feet.

The swineherd and his wife did not like him at all; in fact, they disliked him because he was so much prettier and so much brighter than their own clumsy children. And the children did not like him, because they were ill natured and only liked themselves.

So as he grew older year by year, the poor little Prince was more and more lonely. He had no one to play with, and was obliged to be always by himself. He dressed only in the coarsest and roughest clothes; he seldom had enough to eat, and he slept on straw in a loft under the roof of the swineherd's hut. But all this did not prevent his being strong and rosy and active. He was as fleet as the wind, and he had a voice as sweet as a bird's; he had lovely sparkling eyes, and bright golden hair; and he had so kind a heart that he would not have done a wrong or cruel thing for the world. As soon as he was big enough, the swineherd made him go out into the forest every day to take care of the swine. He was obliged to keep them together in one place, and if any of them ran away into the forest, Prince Fairyfoot was beaten. And as the swine were very wild and unruly, he was very often beaten, because it was almost impossible to keep them from wandering off; and when they ran away, they ran so fast, and through places so tangled, that it was almost impossible to follow them.

The forest in which he had to spend the long days was a very beautiful one, however, and he could take pleasure in that. It was a forest so great that it was like a world in itself. There were in it strange, splendid trees, the branches of which interlocked overhead, and when their many leaves moved and rustled, it seemed as if they were whispering secrets. There were bright, swift, strange birds, that flew about in the deep golden sunshine, and when they rested on the boughs, they, too, seemed telling one another secrets. There was a bright, clear brook, with water as sparkling and pure as crystal, and with shining shells and pebbles of all colours lying in the gold and silver sand at the bottom. Prince Fairyfoot always thought the brook knew the forest's secret also, and sang it softly to the flowers as it ran along. And as for the flowers, they were beautiful; they grew as thickly as if they had been a carpet, and under them was another carpet of lovely green moss. The trees and the birds, and the brook and the flowers were Prince Fairyfoot's friends. He loved them, and never was very lonely when he was with them; and if his swine had not run away so often, and if the swineherd had not beaten him so much, sometimes—indeed, nearly all summer—he would have been almost happy. He used to lie on the fragrant carpet of flowers and moss and listen to the soft sound of the running water, and to the whispering of the waving leaves, and to the songs of the birds; and he would wonder what they were saying to one another, and if it were true, as the swineherd's children said, that the great forest was full of fairies. And then he would pretend it was true, and would tell himself stories about them, and make believe they were his friends, and that they came to talk to him and let him love them. He wanted to love something or somebody, and he had nothing to love—not even a little dog.

One day he was resting under a great green tree, feeling really quite happy because everything was so beautiful. He had even made a little song to chime in with the brook's, and he was singing it softly and sweetly, when suddenly, as he lifted his curly, golden head to look about him, he saw that all his swine were gone. He sprang to his feet, feeling very much frightened, and he whistled and called, but he heard nothing. He could not imagine how they had all disappeared so quietly, without making any sound; but not one of them was anywhere to be seen. Then his poor little heart began to beat fast with trouble and anxiety. He ran here and there; he looked through the bushes and under the trees; he ran, and ran, and ran, and called and whistled, and searched; but nowhere—nowhere was one of those swine to be found! He searched for them for hours, going deeper and deeper into the forest than he had ever been before. He saw strange trees and strange flowers, and heard strange sounds: and at last the sun began to go down, and he knew he would soon be left in the dark. His little feet and legs were scratched with brambles, and were so tired that they would scarcely carry him; but he dared not go back to the swineherd's hut without finding the swine. The only comfort he had on all the long way was that the little brook had run by his side, and sung its song to him; and sometimes he had stopped and bathed his hot face in it, and had said, "Oh, little brook! you are so kind to me! You are my friend, I know. I would be so lonely without you!"

When at last the sun did go down, Prince Fairyfoot had wandered so far that he did not know where he was, and he was so tired that he threw himself down by the brook, and hid his face in the flowery moss, and said, "Oh, little brook! I am so tired I can go no further; and I can never find them!"

While he was lying there in despair, he heard a sound in the air above him, and looked up to see what it was. It sounded like a little bird in some trouble. And, surely enough, there was a huge hawk darting after a plump little brown bird with a red breast. The little bird was uttering sharp frightened cries, and Prince Fairyfoot felt so sorry for it that he sprang up and tried to drive the hawk away. The little bird saw him at once, and straightway flew to him, and Fairyfoot covered it with his cap. And then the hawk flew away in a great rage.

When the hawk was gone, Fairyfoot sat down again and lifted his cap, expecting, of course, to see the brown bird with the red breast. But, instead of a bird, out stepped a little man, not much higher than your little finger—a plump little man in a brown suit with a bright red vest, and with a cocked hat on.

"Why," exclaimed Fairyfoot, "I'm surprised!"

"So am I," said the little man, cheerfully. "I never was more surprised in my life, except when my great-aunt's grandmother got into such a rage, and changed me into a robin-redbreast. I tell you, that surprised me!"

"I should think it might," said Fairyfoot. "Why did she do it?"

"Mad," answered the little man—"that was what was the matter with her. She was always losing her temper like that, and turning people into awkward things, and then being sorry for it, and not being able to change them back again. If you are a fairy, you have to be careful. If you'll believe me, that woman once turned her second-cousin's sister-in-law into a mushroom, and somebody picked her, and she was made into catsup, which is a thing no man likes to have happen in his family!"

"Of course not," said Fairyfoot, politely.

"The difficulty is," said the little man, "that some fairies don't graduate. They learn to turn people into things, but they don't learn how to unturn them; and then, when they get mad in their families—you know how it is about getting mad in families—there is confusion. Yes, seriously, confusion arises. It arises. That was the way with my great-aunt's grandmother. She was not a cultivated old person, and she did not know how to unturn people, and now you see the result. Quite accidentally I trod on her favorite corn; she got mad and changed me into a robin, and regretted it ever afterward. I could only become myself again by a kind-hearted person's saving me from a great danger. You are that person. Give me your hand."

Fairyfoot held out his hand. The little man looked at it.

"On second thought," he said, "I can't shake it—it's too large. I'll sit on it, and talk to you."

With these words, he hopped upon Fairyfoot's hand, and sat down, smiling and clasping his own hands about his tiny knees.

"I declare, it's delightful not to be a robin," he said. "Had to go about picking up worms, you know. Disgusting business. I always did hate worms. I never ate them myself—I drew the line there; but I had to get them for my family."

Suddenly he began to giggle, and to hug his knees up tight.

"Do you wish to know what I'm laughing at?" he asked Fairyfoot.

"Yes," Fairyfoot answered.

The little man giggled more than ever.

"I'm thinking about my wife," he said—"the one I had when I was a robin. A nice rage she'll be in when I don't come home to-night! She'll have to hustle around and pick up worms for herself, and for the children too, and it serves her right. She had a temper that would embitter the life of a crow, much more a simple robin. I wore myself to skin and bone taking care of her and her brood, and how I did hate 'em!—bare, squawking things, always with their throats gaping open. They seemed to think a parent's sole duty was to bring worms for them."

"It must have been unpleasant," said Fairyfoot.

"It was more than that," said the little man; "it used to make my feathers stand on end. There was the nest, too! Fancy being changed into a robin, and being obliged to build a nest at a moment's notice! I never felt so ridiculous in my life. How was I to know how to build a nest! And the worst of it was the way she went on about it."

"She!" said Fairyfoot.

"Oh, her, you know," replied the little man, ungrammatically, "my wife. She'd always been a robin, and she knew how to build a nest; she liked to order me about, too—she was one of that kind. But, of course, I wasn't going to own that I didn't know anything about nest-building. I could never have done anything with her in the world if I'd let her think she knew as much as I did. So I just put things together in a way of my own, and built a nest that would have made you weep! The bottom fell out of it the first night. It nearly killed me."

"Did you fall out, too?" inquired Fairyfoot.

"Oh, no," answered the little man. "I meant that it nearly killed me to think the eggs weren't in it at the time."

"What did you do about the nest?" asked Fairyfoot.

The little man winked in the most improper manner.

"Do?" he said. "I got mad, of course, and told her that if she hadn't interfered, it wouldn't have happened; said it was exactly like a hen to fly around giving advice and unsettling one's mind, and then complain if things weren't right. I told her she might build the nest herself, if she thought she could build a better one. She did it, too!" And he winked again.

"Was it a better one?" asked Fairyfoot.

The little man actually winked a third time. "It may surprise you to hear that it was," he replied; "but it didn't surprise me. By-the-by," he added, with startling suddenness, "what's your name, and what's the matter with you?"

"My name is Prince Fairyfoot," said the boy, "and I have lost my master's swine."

"My name," said the little man, "is Robin Goodfellow, and I'll find them for you."

He had a tiny scarlet silk pouch hanging at his girdle, and he put his hand into it and drew forth the smallest golden whistle you ever saw.

"Blow that," he said, giving it to Fairyfoot, "and take care that you don't swallow it. You are such a tremendous creature!"

Fairyfoot took the whistle and put it very delicately to his lips. He blew, and there came from it a high, clear sound that seemed to pierce the deepest depths of the forest.

"Blow again," commanded Robin Goodfellow.

Again Prince Fairyfoot blew, and again the pure clear sound rang through the trees, and the next instant he heard a loud rushing and tramping and squeaking and grunting, and all the great drove of swine came tearing through the bushes and formed themselves into a circle and stood staring at him as if waiting to be told what to do next.

"Oh, Robin Goodfellow, Robin Goodfellow!" cried Fairyfoot, "how grateful I am to you!"

"Not as grateful as I am to you," said Robin Goodfellow. "But for you I should be disturbing that hawk's digestion at the present moment, instead of which, here I am, a respectable fairy once more, and my late wife (though I ought not to call her that, for goodness knows she was early enough hustling me out of my nest before daybreak, with the unpleasant proverb about the early bird catching the worm!)—I suppose I should say my early wife—is at this juncture a widow. Now, where do you live?"

Fairyfoot told him, and told him also about the swineherd, and how it happened that, though he was a prince, he had to herd swine and live in the forest.

"Well, well," said Robin Goodfellow, "that is a disagreeable state of affairs. Perhaps I can make it rather easier for you. You see that is a fairy whistle."

"I thought so," said Fairyfoot.

"Well," continued Robin Goodfellow, "you can always call your swine with it, so you will never be beaten again. Now, are you ever lonely?"

"Sometimes I am very lonely indeed," answered the Prince. "No one cares for me, though I think the brook is sometimes sorry, and tries to tell me things."

"Of course," said Robin. "They all like you. I've heard them say so."

"Oh, have you?" cried Fairyfoot, joyfully.

"Yes; you never throw stones at the birds, or break the branches of the trees, or trample on the flowers when you can help it."

"The birds sing to me," said Fairyfoot, "and the trees seem to beckon to me and whisper; and when I am very lonely, I lie down in the grass and look into the eyes of the flowers and talk to them. I would not hurt one of them for all the world!"

"Humph!" said Robin, "you are a rather good little fellow. Would you like to go to a party?"

"A party!" said Fairyfoot. "What is that?"

"This sort of thing," said Robin; and he jumped up and began to dance around and to kick up his heels gaily in the palm of Fairyfoot's hand. "Wine, you know, and cake, and all sorts of fun. It begins at twelve to-night, in a place the fairies know of, and it lasts until just two minutes and three seconds and a half before daylight. Would you like to come?"

"Oh," cried Fairyfoot, "I should be so happy if I might!"

"Well, you may," said Robin; "I'll take you. They'll be delighted to see any friend of mine, I'm a great favourite; of course, you can easily imagine that. It was a great blow to them when I was changed; such a loss, you know. In fact, there were several lady fairies, who—but no matter." And he gave a slight cough, and began to arrange his necktie with a disgracefully consequential air, though he was trying very hard not to look conceited; and while he was endeavouring to appear easy and gracefully careless, he began accidentally to hum, "See the Conquering Hero Comes," which was not the right tune under the circumstances.

"But for you," he said next, "I couldn't have given them the relief and pleasure of seeing me this evening. And what ecstasy it will be to them, to be sure! I shouldn't be surprised if it broke up the whole thing. They'll faint so— for joy, you know—just at first—that is, the ladies will. The men won't like it at all; and I don't blame 'em. I suppose I shouldn't like it—to see another fellow sweep all before him. That's what I do; I sweep all before me." And he waved his hand in such a fine large gesture that he overbalanced himself, and turned a somersault. But he jumped up after it quite undisturbed.

"You'll see me do it to-night," he said, knocking the dents out of his hat—"sweep all before me." Then he put his hat on, and his hands on his hips, with a swaggering, man-of-society air. "I say," he said, "I'm glad you're going. I should like you to see it."

"And I should like to see it," replied Fairyfoot.

"Well," said Mr. Goodfellow, "you deserve it, though that's saying a great deal. You've restored me to them. But for you, even if I'd escaped that hawk, I should have had to spend the night in that beastly robin's nest, crowded into a corner by those squawking things, and domineered over by her! I wasn't made for that! I'm superior to it. Domestic life doesn't suit me. I was made for society. I adorn it. She never appreciated me. She couldn't soar to it. When I think of the way she treated me," he exclaimed, suddenly getting into a rage, "I've a great mind to turn back into a robin and peck her head off!"

"Would you like to see her now?" asked Fairyfoot, innocently.

Mr. Goodfellow glanced behind him in great haste, and suddenly sat down.

"No, no!" he exclaimed in a tremendous hurry; "by no means! She has no delicacy. And she doesn't deserve to see me. And there's a violence and uncertainty about her movements which is annoying beyond anything you can imagine. No, I don't want to see her! I'll let her go unpunished for the present. Perhaps it's punishment enough for her to be deprived of me. Just pick up your cap, won't you? and if you see any birds lying about, throw it at them, robins particularly."

"I think I must take the swine home, if you'll excuse me," said Fairyfoot, "I'm late now."

"Well, let me sit on your shoulder and I'll go with you and show you a short way home," said Goodfellow; "I know all about it, so you needn't think about yourself again. In fact, we'll talk about the party. Just blow your whistle, and the swine will go ahead."

Fairyfoot did so, and the swine rushed through the forest before them, and Robin Goodfellow perched himself on the Prince's shoulder, and chatted as they went.

It had taken Fairyfoot hours to reach the place where he found Robin, but somehow it seemed to him only a very short time before they came to the open place near the swineherd's hut; and the path they had walked in had been so pleasant and flowery that it had been delightful all the way.

"Now," said Robin when they stopped, "if you will come

here to-night at twelve o'clock, when the moon shines under this tree, you will find me waiting for you. Now I'm going. Good-bye!" And he was gone before the last word was quite finished.

Fairyfoot went towards the hut, driving the swine before him, and suddenly he saw the swineherd come out of his house, and stand staring stupidly at the pigs. He was a very coarse, hideous man, with bristling yellow hair, and little eyes, and a face rather like a pig's, and he always looked stupid, but just now he looked more stupid than ever. He seemed dumb with surprise.

"What's the matter with the swine?" he asked in his hoarse voice, which was rather piglike, too.

"I don't know," answered Fairyfoot, feeling a little alarmed. "What *is* the matter with them?"

'They are four times fatter, and five times bigger, and six times cleaner, and seven times heavier, and eight times handsomer than they were when you took them out," the swineherd said.

"I've done nothing to them," said Fairyfoot. "They ran away, but they came back again."

The swineherd went lumbering back into the hut, and called his wife.

"Come and look at the swine," he said.

And then the woman came out, and stared first at the swine and then at Fairyfoot.

"He has been with the fairies," she said at last to her husband; "or it is because he is a king's son. We must treat him better if he can do wonders like that."

Part II

In went the shepherd's wife, and she prepared quite a good supper for Fairyfoot and gave it to him. But Fairyfoot was scarcely hungry at all; he was so eager for the night to come, so that he might see the fairies. When he went to his loft under the roof, he thought at first that he could not sleep; but suddenly his hand touched the fairy whistle and he fell asleep at once, and did not waken again until a moonbeam fell brightly upon his face and aroused him. Then he jumped up and ran to the hole in the wall to look out, and he saw that the hour had come, and the moon was so low in the sky that its slanting light had crept under the oak-tree.

He slipped downstairs so lightly that his master heard nothing, and then he found himself out in the beautiful night with the moonlight so bright that it was lighter than daytime. And there was Robin Goodfellow waiting for him under the tree! He was so finely dressed that, for a moment, Fairyfoot scarcely knew him. His suit was made out of the purple velvet petals of a pansy, which was far finer than any ordinary velvet, and he wore plumes and tassels, and a ruffle around his neck, and in his belt was thrust a tiny sword, not half as big as the finest needle.

"Take me on your shoulder," he said to Fairyfoot, "and I will show you the way."

Fairyfoot took him up, and they went their way through the forest. And the strange part of it was that though Fairyfoot thought he knew all the forest by heart, every path they took was new to him, and more beautiful than anything he had ever seen before. The moonlight seemed to grow brighter and purer at every step, and the sleeping flowers sweeter and lovelier, and the moss greener and thicker. Fairyfoot felt so happy and gay that he forgot he had ever been sad and lonely in his life.

Robin Goodfellow, too, seemed to be in very good spirits. He related a great many stories to Fairyfoot, and, singularly enough, they were all about himself and divers and sundry fairy ladies who had been so very much attached to him that he scarcely expected to find them alive at the present moment. He felt quite sure they must have died of grief in his absence.

"I have caused a great deal of trouble in the course of my life," he said, regretfully, shaking his head. "I have sometimes wished I could avoid it, but that is impossible.

Ahem! When my great-aunt's grandmother rashly and inopportunely changed me into a robin, I was having a little flirtation with a little creature who was really quite attractive. I might have decided to engage myself to her. She was very charming. Her name was Gauzita. To-morrow I shall go and place flowers on her tomb."

"I thought fairies never died," said Fairyfoot.

"Only on rare occasions, and only from love," answered Robin. "They needn't die unless they wish to. They have been known to do it through love. They frequently wish they hadn't afterward—in fact, invariably—and then they can come to life again. But Gauzita——"

"Are you quite sure she is dead?" asked Fairyfoot.

"Sure!" cried Mr. Goodfellow, in wild indignation, "why, she hasn't seen me for a couple of years. I've moulted twice since last we met. I congratulate myself that she didn't see me then," he added, in a lower voice. "Of course she's dead," he added, with solemn emphasis; "as dead as a door nail."

Just then Fairyfoot heard some enchanting sounds, faint, but clear. They were the sounds of delicate music and of tiny laughter, like the ringing of fairy bells.

"Ah!" said Robin Goodfellow, "there they are! But it seems to me they are rather gay, considering they have not seen me for so long. Turn into the path."

Almost immediately they found themselves in a beautiful little dell, filled with moonlight, and with glittering stars in the cup of every flower; for there were thousands of dewdrops, and every dewdrop shone like a star. There were also crowds and crowds of tiny men and women, all beautiful, all dressed in brilliant, delicate dresses, all laughing or dancing or feasting at the little tables, which were loaded with every dainty the most fastidious fairy could wish for.

"Now," said Robin Goodfellow, "you shall see me sweep all before me. Put me down."

Fairyfoot put him down, and stood and watched him while he walked forward with a very grand manner. He went straight to the gayest and largest group he could see. It was a group of gentlemen fairies, who were crowding around a lily of the valley, on the bent stem of which a tiny lady fairy was sitting, airily swaying herself to and fro, and laughing and chatting with all her admirers at once.

She seemed to be enjoying herself immensely; indeed, it was disgracefully plain that she was having a great deal of fun. One gentleman fairy was fanning her, one was holding her programme, one had her bouquet, another her little scent bottle, and those who had nothing to hold for her were scowling furiously at the rest. It was evident that she was very popular, and that she did not object to it at all; in fact, the way her eyes sparkled and danced was distinctly reprehensible.

"You have engaged to dance the next waltz with every one of us!" said one of her adorers. "How are you going to do it?"

"Did I engage to dance with all of you?" she said, giving her lily stem the sauciest little swing, which set all the bells ringing. "Well, I am not going to dance it with all."

"Not with *me?*" the admirer with the fan whispered in her ear.

She gave him the most delightful little look, just to make him believe she wanted to dance with him but really couldn't. Robin Goodfellow saw her. And then she smiled sweetly upon all the rest, every one of them. Robin Goodfellow saw that, too.

"I am going to sit here and look at you, and let you talk to me," she said. "I do so enjoy brilliant conversation."

All the gentlemen fairies were so much elated by this that they began to brighten up, and settle their ruffs, and fall into graceful attitudes, and think of sparkling things to say; because every one of them knew, from the glance of her eyes in his direction, that he was one whose conversation was brilliant; every one knew there could be no mistake about its being himself that she meant. The way she looked just proved it. Altogether it was more than Robin Goodfellow could stand, for it was Gauzita who was deporting herself in this unaccountable manner, swinging on lily stems, and "going on," so to speak, with several parties at once, in a way to chill the blood of any proper young lady fairy—who hadn't any partner at all. It was Gauzita herself.

He made his way into the very centre of the group.

"Gauzita!" he said. He thought, of course, she would drop right off her lily stem; but she didn't. She simply stopped swinging a moment, and stared at him.

"Gracious!" she exclaimed. "And who are you?"

"Who am I?" cried Mr. Goodfellow, severely. "Don't you remember me?"

"No," she said, coolly; "I don't, not in the least."

Robin Goodfellow almost gasped for breath. He had never met with anything so outrageous in his life.

"You don't remember *me?*" he cried. "*Me!* Why, it's impossible!"

"Is it?" said Gauzita, with a touch of dainty impudence. "What's your name?"

Robin Goodfellow was almost paralyzed. Gauzita took up a midget of an eyeglass which she had dangling from a thread of a gold chain, and she stuck it in her eye and tilted her impertinent little chin and looked him over. Not that she was near-sighted—not a bit of it; it was just one of her tricks and manners.

"Dear me!" she said, "you do look a trifle familiar. It isn't, it can't be, Mr.——, Mr.——," then she turned to the adorer, who held her fan, "it can't be Mr. ——, the one who was changed into a robin, you know," she said. "Such a ridiculous thing to be changed into! What was his name?"

"Oh, yes! I know whom you mean. Mr. ——, ah—Good-fellow!" said the fairy with the fan.

"So it was," she said, looking Robin over again. "And he has been pecking at trees and things, and hopping in and out of nests ever since, I suppose. How absurd! And we have been enjoying ourselves so much since he went away! I think I never *did* have so lovely a time as I have had during these last two years. I began to know you," she added, in a kindly tone, "just about the time he went away."

"You have been enjoying yourself?" almost shrieked Robin Goodfellow.

"Well," said Gauzita, in unexcusable slang, "I must smile." And she did smile.

"And nobody has pined away and died?" cried Robin.

"I haven't," said Gauzita, swinging herself and ringing her bells again. "I really haven't had time."

Robin Goodfellow turned around and rushed out of the group. He regarded this as insulting. He went back to Fairyfoot in such a hurry that he tripped on his sword and fell, and rolled over so many times that Fairyfoot had to stop him and pick him up.

"Is she dead?" asked Fairyfoot.

"No," said Robin; "she isn't."

He sat down on a small mushroom and clasped his hands about his knees and looked mad—just mad. Angry or indignant wouldn't express it.

"I have a great mind to go and be a misanthrope," he said.

"Oh! I wouldn't," said Fairyfoot. He didn't know what a misanthrope was, but he thought it must be something unpleasant.

"Wouldn't you?" said Robin, looking up at him.

"No," answered Fairyfoot.

"Well," said Robin, "I guess I won't. Let's go and have some fun. They are all that way. You can't depend on any of them. Never trust one of them. I believe that creature has been engaged as much as twice since I left. By a singular coincidence," he added, "I have been married twice myself—but, of course, that's different. I'm a man, you know, and—well, it's different. We won't dwell on it. Let's go and dance. But wait a minute first." He took a little bottle from his pocket.

"If you remain the size you are," he continued, "you will tread on whole sets of lancers and destroy entire germans. If you drink this, you will become as small as we are; and then, when you are going home, I will give you something to make you large again." Fairyfoot drank from the little flagon, and immediately he felt himself growing smaller and smaller until at last he was as small as his companion.

"Now, come on," said Robin.

On they went and joined the fairies, and they danced and played fairy games and feasted on fairy dainties, and were so gay and happy that Fairyfoot was wild with joy. Everybody made him welcome and seemed to like him, and the lady fairies were simply delightful, especially Gauzita, who took a great fancy to him. Just before the sun rose, Robin gave him something from another flagon, and he grew large again, and two minutes and three seconds and a half before daylight the ball broke up, and Robin took him home and left him, promising to call for him the next night.

Every night throughout the whole summer the same thing happened. At midnight he went to the fairies' dance; and at two minutes and three seconds and a half before dawn he came home. He was never lonely any more, because all day long he could think of what pleasure he would have when the night came; and, besides that, all the fairies were his friends. But when the summer was coming to an end, Robin Goodfellow said to him: "This is our last dance—at least it will be our last for some time. At this time of the year we always go back to our own country, and we don't return until spring."

This made Fairyfoot very sad. He did not know how he could bear to be left alone again, but he knew it could not be helped; so he tried to be as cheerful as possible, and he went to the final festivities, and enjoyed himself more than ever before, and Gauzita gave him a tiny ring for a parting gift. But the next night, when Robin did not come for him, he felt very lonely indeed, and the next day he was so sorrowful that he wandered far away into the forest, in the hope of finding something to cheer him a little.

He wandered so far that he became very tired and thirsty, and he was just making up his mind to go home, when he thought he heard the sound of falling water. It seemed to come from behind a thicket of climbing roses; and he went towards the place and pushed the branches aside a little, so that he could look through. What he saw was a great surprise to him. Though it was the end of summer, inside the thicket the roses were blooming in thousands all around a pool as clear as crystal, into which the sparkling water fell from a hole in the rock above. It was the most beautiful, clear pool that Fairyfoot had ever seen, and he pressed his way through the rose branches, and, entering the circle they inclosed, he knelt by the water and drank.

Almost instantly his feeling of sadness left him, and he felt quite happy and refreshed. He stretched himself on the thick perfumed moss, and listened to the tinkling of the water, and it was not long before he fell asleep.

When he awakened the moon was shining, the pool sparkled like a silver plaque crusted with diamonds, and two nightingales were singing in the branches over his head. And the next moment he found out that he understood their language just as plainly as if they had been human beings instead of birds. The water with which he had quenched his thirst was enchanted, and had given him this new power.

"Poor boy!" said one nightingale, "he looks tired; I wonder where he came from."

"Why, my dear," said the other, "is it possible you don't know that he is Prince Fairyfoot?"

"What!" said the first nightingale—"the King of Stumpinghame's son, who was born with small feet?"

"Yes," said the second. "And the poor child has lived in the forest, keeping the swineherd's pigs ever since. And he is a very nice boy, too—never throws stones at birds or robs nests."

"What a pity he doesn't know about the pool where the red berries grow!" said the first nightingale.

Part III

"What pool—and what red berries?" asked the second nightingale.

"Why, my dear," said the first, "is it possible you don't know about the pool where the red berries grow—the pool where the poor, dear Princess Goldenhair met with her misfortune?"

"Never heard of it," said the second nightingale, rather crossly.

"Well," explained the other, "you have to follow the brook for a day and three-quarters, and then take all the paths to the left until you come to the pool. It is very ugly and muddy, and bushes with red berries on them grow around it."

"Well, what of that?" said her companion; "and what happened to the Princess Goldenhair?"

"Don't you know that, either?" exclaimed her friend.

"No."

"Ah!" said the first nightingale, "it was very sad. She went out with her father, the King, who had a hunting party; and she lost her way, and wandered on until she came to the pool. Her poor little feet were so hot that she took off her gold-embroidered satin slippers, and put them into the water—her feet, not the slippers—and the next minute they began to grow and grow, and to get larger and larger, until they were so immense she could hardly walk at all; and though all the physicians in the kingdom have tried to make them smaller, nothing can be done, and she is perfectly unhappy."

"What a pity she doesn't know about this pool!" said the other bird. "If she just came here and bathed them three times in the water, they would be smaller and more beautiful than ever, and she would be more lovely than she has ever been."

"It is a pity," said her companion; "but, you know, if we once let people know what this water will do, we should be overrun with creatures bathing themselves beautiful, and trampling our moss and tearing down our rose-trees, and we should never have any peace."

"That is true," agreed the other.

Very soon after they flew away, and Fairyfoot was left alone. He had been so excited while they were talking that he had been hardly able to lie still. He was so sorry for the Princess Goldenhair, and so glad for himself. Now he could find his way to the pool with the red berries, and he could bathe his feet in it until they were large enough to satisfy Stumpinghame; and he could go back to his father's court, and his parents would perhaps be fond of him. But he had so good a heart that he could not think of being happy himself and letting others remain unhappy, when he could help them. So the first thing was to find the Princess Goldenhair and tell her about the nightingales' fountain. But how was he to find her? The nightingales had not told him. He was very much troubled, indeed. How was he to find her?

Suddenly, quite suddenly, he thought of the ring Gauzita had given him. When she had given it to him she had made an odd remark.

"When you wish to go anywhere," she had said, "hold it in your hand, turn around twice with closed eyes, and something queer will happen."

He had thought it was one of her little jokes, but now it occurred to him that at least he might try what would happen. So he rose up, held the ring in his hand, closed his eyes, and turned around twice.

What did happen was that he began to walk, not very fast, but still passing along as if he were moving rapidly. He did not know where he was going, but he guessed that the ring did, and that if he obeyed it, he should find the Princes Goldenhair. He went on and on, not getting in the least tired, until about daylight he found himself under a great tree, and on the ground beneath it was spread a delightful breakfast, which he knew was for him. He sat down and ate it, and then got up again and went on his way once more. Before noon he had left the forest behind him, and was in a strange country. He knew it was not Stumpinghame, because the people had not large feet. But they all had sad faces, and once or twice, when he passed groups of them who were talking, he heard them speak of the Princess Goldenhair, as if they were sorry for her and could not enjoy themselves while such a misfortune rested upon her.

"So sweet and lovely and kind a princess!" they said; "and it really seems as if she would never be any better."

The sun was just setting when Fairyfoot came in sight of the palace. It was built of white marble, and had beautiful pleasure-grounds about it, but somehow there seemed to be a settled gloom in the air. Fairyfoot had entered the great pleasure-garden, and was wondering where it would be best to go first, when he saw a lovely white fawn, with a golden collar about its neck, come bounding over the flower-beds, and he heard, at a little distance, a sweet voice, saying, sorrowfully, "Come back, my fawn; I cannot run and play with you as I once used to. Do not leave me, my little friend."

And soon from behind the trees came a line of beautiful girls, walking two by two, all very slowly; and at the head of the line, first of all, came the loveliest princess in the world, dressed softly in pure white, with a wreath of lilies on her long golden hair, which fell almost to the hem of her white gown.

She had so fair and tender a young face, and her large, soft eyes, yet looked so sorrowful, that Fairyfoot loved her in a moment, and he knelt on one knee, taking off his cap and bending his head until his own golden hair almost hid his face.

"Beautiful Princess Goldenhair, beautiful and sweet Princess, may I speak to you?" he said.

The Princess stopped and looked at him, and answered him softly. It surprised her to see one so poorly dressed kneeling before her, in her palace gardens, among the brilliant flowers; but she always spoke softly to everyone.

"What is there that I can do for you, my friend?" she said.

"Beautiful Princess," answered Fairyfoot, blushing, "I hope very much that I may be able to do something for you."

"For me!" she exclaimed. "Thank you, friend; what is it you can do? Indeed, I need a help I am afraid no one can ever give me."

"Gracious and fairest lady," said Fairyfoot, "it is that help I think—nay, I am sure—that I bring to you."

"Oh!" said the sweet Princess. "You have a kind face and most true eyes, and when I look at you—I do not know why it is, but I feel a little happier. What is it you would say to me?"

Still kneeling before her, still bending his head modestly, and still blushing, Fairyfoot told his story. He told her of his own sadness and loneliness, and of why he was considered so terrible a disgrace to his family. He told her about the fountain of the nightingales and what he had heard there and how he had journeyed through the forests, and beyond it into her own country, to find her. And while he told it, her beautiful face changed from red to white, and her hands closely clasped themselves together.

"Oh!" she said, when he had finished, "I know that this is true from the kind look in your eyes, and I shall be happy again. And how can I thank you for being so good to a poor little princess whom you had never seen?"

"Only let me see you happy once more, most sweet Princess," answered Fairyfoot, "and that will be all I desire—only if, perhaps, I might once—kiss your hand."

She held out her hand to him with so lovely a look in her soft eyes that he felt happier than he had ever been before, even at the fairy dances. This was a different kind of happiness. Her hand was as white as a dove's wing and as soft as a dove's breast. "Come," she said, "let us go at once to the King.'

Within a few minutes the whole palace was in an uproar of excitement. Preparations were made to go to the fountain of the nightingales immediately. Remembering what the birds had said about not wishing to be disturbed, Fairyfoot asked the King to take only a small party. So no one was to go but the King himself, the Princess, in a covered chair carried by two bearers, the Lord High Chamberlain, two Maids of Honour, and Fairyfoot.

Before morning they were on their way, and the day after they reached the thicket of roses, and Fairyfoot pushed aside the branches and led the way into the dell.

The Princess Goldenhair sat down upon the edge of the pool and put her feet into it. In two minutes they began to look smaller. She bathed them once, twice, three times, and, as the nightingales had said, they became smaller and more beautiful than ever. As for the Princess herself, she really could not be more beautiful than she had been; but the Lord High Chamberlain, who had been an exceedingly ugly old gentleman, after washing his face, became so young and handsome that the First Maid of Honour immediately fell in love with him. Whereupon she washed her face, and became so beautiful that he fell in love with her, and they were engaged upon the spot.

The Princess could not find any words to tell Fairyfoot how grateful she was and how happy. She could only look at him again and again with her soft, radiant eyes, and again and again give him her hand that he might kiss it.

She was so sweet and gentle that Fairyfoot could not bear the thought of leaving her; and when the King begged him to return to the palace with them and live there always, he was more glad than I can tell you. To be near this lovely Princess, to be her friend, to love and serve her and look at her every day, was such happiness that he wanted nothing more. But first he wished to visit his father and mother and sisters and brothers in Stumpinghame! so the King and Princess and their attendants went with him to the pool where the red berries grew; and after he had bathed his feet in the water they were so large that Stumpinghame contained nothing like them, even the King's and Queen's seeming small in comparison. And when, a few days later, he arrived at the

Stumpingham Palace, attended in great state by the magnificent retinue with which the father of the Princess Goldenhair had provided him, he was received with unbounded rapture by his parents. The King and Queen felt that to have a son with feet of such a size was something to be proud of, indeed. They could not admire him sufficiently, although the whole country was illuminated, and feasting continued throughout his visit.

But though he was glad to be no more a disgrace to his family, it cannot be said that he enjoyed the size of his feet very much on his own account. Indeed, he much preferred being Prince Fairyfoot, as fleet as the wind and as light as a young deer, and he was quite glad to go to the fountain of the nightingales after his visit was at an end, and bathe his feet small again, and to return to the palace of the Princess Goldenhair with the soft and tender eyes. There everyone loved him, and he loved everyone, and was four times as happy as the day is long.

He loved the Princess more dearly every day, and, of course, as soon as they were old enough, they were married. And of course, too, they used to go in the summer to the forest, and dance in the moonlight with the fairies, who adored them both.

When they went to visit Stumpinghame, they always bathed their feet in the pool of the red berries; and when they returned, they made them small again in the fountain of the nightingales.

They were always great friends with Robin Goodfellow, and he was always very confidential with them about Gauzita, who continued to be as pretty and saucy as ever.

"Some of these days," he used to say, severely, "I'll marry another fairy, and see how she'll like that—to see someone else basking in my society! *I'll* get even with her!"

But he *never* did.

The Proud Little Grain of Wheat

There once was a little grain of wheat which was very proud indeed. The first thing it remembered was being very much crowded and jostled by a great many other grains of wheat, all living in the same sack in the granary. It was quite dark in the sack, and no one could move about, and so there was nothing to be done but to sit still and talk and think. The proud little grain of wheat talked a great deal, but did not think quite so much, while its next neighbour thought a great deal and only talked when it was asked questions it could not answer. It used to say that when it thought a great deal it could remember things which it seemed to have heard a long time ago.

"What is the use of our staying here so long doing nothing, and never being seen by anybody?" the proud little grain once asked.

"I don't know," the learned grain replied. "I don't know the answer to that. Ask me another."

"Why can't I sing like the birds that build their nests in the roof? I should like to sing, instead of sitting here in the dark."

"Because you have no voice," said the learned grain.

This was a very good answer indeed.

"Why didn't someone give me a voice, then—why didn't they?" said the proud little grain, getting very cross.

The learned grain thought for several minutes.

"There might be two answers to that," she said at last. "One might be that nobody had a voice to spare, and the other might be that you have nowhere to put one if it were given to you."

"Everybody is better off than I am," said the proud little grain. "The birds can fly and sing, the children can play and shout. I am sure I can get no rest for their shouting and playing. There are two little boys who make enough noise to deafen the whole sackful of us."

"Ah! I know them," said the learned grain. "And it's true they are noisy. Their names are Lionel and Vivian. There is a thin place in the side of the sack, through which I can see them. I would rather stay where I am than have to do all they do. They have long yellow hair, and when they stand on their heads the straw sticks in it and they look very curious. I heard a strange thing through listening to them the other day."

"What was it?" asked the proud grain.

"They were playing in the straw, and someone came in to them—it was a lady who had brought them something on a plate. They began to dance and shout: 'It's cake! It's cake! Nice little mamma for bringing us cake.' And then they each sat down with a piece and began to take great bites out of it. I shuddered to think of it afterward."

"Why?"

"Well, you know they are always asking questions, and they began to ask questions of their mamma, who lay down in the straw near them. She seemed to be used to it. These are the questions Vivian asked:

"'Who made the cake?'

"'The cook.'

"'Who made the cook?'

"'God.'

"'What did He make her for?'

"'Why didn't He make her white?'

"'Why didn't He make you black?'

"'Did He cut a hole in heaven and drop me through when He made me?'

"'Why didn't it hurt me when I tumbled such a long way?'

"She said she 'didn't know' to all but the two first, and then he asked two more.

"'What is the cake made of?'

"'Flour, sugar, eggs and butter.'

"'What is flour made of?'

"It was the answer to that which made me shudder."

"What was it?" asked the proud grain.

"She said it was made of—wheat! I don't see the advantage of being rich——"

"Was the cake rich?" asked the proud grain.

"Their mother said it was. She said, 'Don't eat it so fast—it is very rich.'"

"Ah!" said the proud grain. "I should like to be rich. It must be very fine to be rich. If I am ever made into cake, I mean to be so rich that no one will dare to eat me at all."

"Ah?" said the learned grain. "I don't think those boys would be afraid to eat you, however rich you were. They are not afraid of richness."

"They'd be afraid of me before they had done with me," said the proud grain. "I am not a common grain of wheat. Wait until I am made into cake. But gracious me! there doesn't seem much prospect of it while we are shut up here. How dark and stuffy it is, and how we are crowded, and what a stupid lot the other grains are! I'm tired of it, I must say."

"We are all in the same sack," said the learned grain, very quietly.

It was a good many days after that, that something happened. Quite early in the morning, a man and a boy came into the granary, and moved the sack of wheat from its place, wakening all the grains from their last nap.

"What is the matter?" said the proud grain. "Who is daring to disturb us?"

"Hush!" whispered the learned grain, in the most solemn manner. "Something is going to happen. Something like this happened to somebody belonging to me long ago. I seem to remember it when I think very hard. I seem to remember something about one of my family being sown."

"What is sown?" demanded the other grain.

"It is being thrown into the earth," began the learned grain.

Oh, what a passion the proud grain got into! "Into the earth?" she shrieked out. "Into the common earth? The earth is nothing but dirt, and I am *not* a common grain of wheat. I won't be sown! I will *not* be sown! How dare anyone sow me against my will! I would rather stay in the sack."

But just as she was saying it, she was thrown out with the learned grain and some others into another dark place, and carried off by the farmer, in spite of her temper; for the farmer could not hear her voice at all, and wouldn't have minded if he had, because he knew she was only a grain of wheat, and ought to be sown, so that some good might come of her.

Well, she was carried out to a large field in the pouch which the farmer wore at his belt. The field had been ploughed, and there was a sweet smell of fresh earth in the air; the sky was a deep, deep blue, but the air was cool and the few leaves on the trees were brown and dry, and looked as if they had been left over from last year.

"Ah!" said the learned grain. "It was just such a day as this when my grandfather, or my father, or somebody else related to me, was sown. I think I remember that it was called Early Spring."

"As for me," said the proud grain, fiercely, "I should like to see the man who would dare to sow me!"

At that very moment, the farmer put his big, brown hand into the bag and threw her, as she thought, at least half a mile from them.

He had not thrown her so far as that, however, and she landed safely in the shadow of a clod of rich earth, which the sun had warmed through and through. She was quite out of breath and very dizzy at first, but in a few seconds she began to feel better and could not help looking around, in spite of her anger, to see if there was anyone near to talk to. But she saw no one, and so began to scold as usual.

"They not only sow me," she called out, "but they throw me all by myself, where I can have no company at all. It is disgraceful."

Then she heard a voice from the other side of the clod. It was the learned grain, who had fallen there when the farmer threw her out of his pouch.

"Don't be angry," it said, "I am here. We are all right so far. Perhaps, when they cover us with the earth, we shall be even nearer to each other than we are now."

"Do you mean to say they will cover us with the earth?" asked the proud grain.

"Yes," was the answer. "And there we shall lie in the dark, and the rain will moisten us, and the sun will warm us, until we grow larger and larger, and at last burst open!"

"Speak for yourself," said the proud grain; "I shall do no such thing!"

But it all happened just as the learned grain had said, which showed what a wise grain it was, and how much it had found out just by thinking hard and remembering all it could.

Before the day was over, they were covered snugly up with the soft, fragrant, brown earth, and there they lay day after day.

One morning, when the proud grain wakened, it found itself wet through and through with rain which had fallen in the night, and the next day the sun shone down and warmed it so that it really began to be afraid that it would be obliged to grow too large for its skin, which felt a little tight for it already.

It said nothing of this to the learned grain, at first, because it was determined not to burst if it could help it; but after the same thing had happened a great many times, it found, one morning, that it really was swelling, and it felt obliged to tell the learned grain about it.

"Well," it said, pettishly, "I suppose you will be glad to hear that you were right. I *am* going to burst. My skin is so tight now that it doesn't fit me at all, and I know I can't stand another warm shower like the last."

"Oh!" said the learned grain, in a quiet way (really learned people always have a quiet way), "I knew I was right, or I shouldn't have said so. I hope you don't find it very uncomfortable. I think I myself shall burst by to-morrow."

"Of course I find it uncomfortable," said the proud grain. "Who wouldn't find it uncomfortable, to be two or three sizes too small for one's self! Pouf! Crack! There I go! I have split up all up my right side, and I must say it's a relief."

"Crack! Pouf! so have I," said the learned grain. "Now we must begin to push up through the earth. I am sure my relation did that."

"Well, I shouldn't mind getting out into the air. It would be a change at least."

So each of them began to push her way through the earth as strongly as she could, and, sure enough, it was not long before the proud grain actually found herself out in the world again, breathing the sweet air, under the blue sky, across which fleecy white clouds were drifting, and swift-winged, happy birds darting.

"It really is a lovely day," were the first words the proud grain said. It couldn't help it. The sunshine was so delightful, and the birds chirped and twittered so merrily in the bare branches, and, more wonderful than all, the great field was brown no longer, but was covered with millions of little, fresh green blades, which trembled and bent their frail bodies before the light wind.

"This *is* an improvement," said the proud grain.

Then there was a little stir in the earth beside it, and up through the brown mould came the learned grain, fresh, bright, green, like the rest.

"I told you I was not a common grain of wheat," said the proud one.

"You are not a grain of wheat at all now," said the learned one, modestly. "You are a blade of wheat, and there are a great many others like you."

"See how green I am!" said the proud blade.

"Yes, you are very green," said its companion. "You will not be so green when you are older."

The proud grain, which must be called a blade now, had plenty of change and company after this. It grew taller and taller every day, and made a great many new acquaintances as the weather grew warmer. These were little gold and green beetles living near it, who often passed it, and now and then stopped to talk a little about their children and their journeys under the soil. Birds dropped down from the sky sometimes to gossip and twitter of the nests they were building in the apple-trees, and the new songs they were learning to sing.

Once, on a very warm day, a great golden butterfly, floating by on his large lovely wings, fluttered down softly and lit on the proud blade, who felt so much prouder when he did it that she trembled for joy.

"He admires me more than all the rest in the field, you see," it said, haughtily. "That is because I am so green."

"If I were you," said the learned blade, in its modest way, "I believe I would not talk so much about being green. People will make such ill-natured remarks when one speaks often of one's self."

"I am above such people," said the proud blade; "I can find nothing more interesting to talk of than myself."

As time went on, it was delighted to find that it grew taller than any other blade in the field, and threw out other blades; and at last there grew out at the top of its stalk ever so many plump, new little grains, all fitting closely together, and wearing tight little green covers.

"Look at me!" it said then. "I am the queen of all the wheat. I have a crown."

"No," said its learned companion. "You are now an ear of wheat."

And in a short time all the other stalks wore the same

kind of crown, and it found out that the learned blade was right, and that it was only an ear, after all.

And now the weather had grown still warmer and the trees were covered with leaves, and the birds sang and built their nests in them and laid their little blue eggs, and in time, wonderful to relate, there came baby birds, that were always opening their mouths for food, and crying "peep, peep," to their fathers and mothers. There were more butterflies floating about on their amber and purple wings, and the gold and green beetles were so busy they had no time to talk.

"Well!" said the proud ear of wheat (you remember it was an ear by this time) to its companion one day. "You see, you were right again. I am not so green as I was. I am turning yellow—but yellow is the colour of gold, and I don't object to looking like gold."

"You will soon be ripe," said its friend.

"And what will happen then?"

"The reaping-machine will come and cut you down, and other strange things will happen."

"There I make a stand," said the proud ear, "I will *not* be cut down."

But it was just as the wise ear said it would be. Not long after a reaping-machine was brought and driven back and forth in the fields, and down went all the wheat ears before the great knives. But it did not hurt the wheat, of course, and only the proud ear felt angry.

"I am the colour of gold," it said, "and yet they have dared to cut me down. What will they do next, I wonder?"

What they did next was to bunch it up with other wheat and tie it and stack it together, and then it was carried in a waggon and laid in the barn.

Then there was a great bustle after a while. The farmer's wife and daughters and her two servants began to work as hard as they could.

"The threshers are coming," they said, "and we must make plenty of things for them to eat."

So they made pies and cakes and bread until their

cupboards were full; and surely enough the threshers did come with the threshing-machine, which was painted red, and went "Puff! puff! puff! rattle! rattle!" all the time. And the proud wheat was threshed out by it, and found itself in grains again and very much out of breath.

"I look almost as I was at first," it said; "only there are so many of me. I am grander than ever now. I was only one grain of wheat at first, and now I am at least fifty."

When it was put into a sack, it managed to get all its grains together in one place, so that it might feel as grand as possible. It was so proud that it felt grand, however much it was knocked about.

It did not lie in the sack very long this time before something else happened. One morning it heard the farmer's wife saying to the coloured boy:

"Take this yere sack of wheat to the mill, Jerry. I want to try it when I make that thar cake for the boarders. Them two children from Washington city are powerful hands for cake."

So Jerry lifted the sack up and threw it over his shoulder, and carried it out into the spring-waggon.

"Now we are going to travel," said the proud wheat. "Don't let us be separated."

At that minute, there were heard two young voices, shouting:—

"Jerry, take us in the waggon! Let us go to mill, Jerry. We want to go to mill."

And these were the very two boys who had played in the granary and made so much noise the summer before. They had grown a little bigger, and their yellow hair was longer, but they looked just as they used to, with their strong little legs and big brown eyes, and their sailor hats set so far back on their heads that it was a wonder they stayed on. And gracious! how they shouted and ran.

"What does yer mar say?" asked Jerry.

"Says we can go!" shouted both at once, as if Jerry had been deaf, which he wasn't at all—quite the contrary.

So Jerry, who was very good-natured, lifted them in,

and cracked his whip, and the horses started off. It was a long ride to the mill, but Lionel and Vivian were not too tired to shout again when they reached it. They shouted at sight of the creek and the big wheel turning round and round slowly, with the water dashing and pouring and foaming over it.

"What turns the wheel?" asked Vivian.

"The water, honey," said Jerry.

"What turns the water?"

"Well now, honey," said Jerry, "you hev me thar. I don't know nuffin 'bout it. Lors-a-massy, what a boy you is fur axin dif'cult questions."

Then he carried the sack in to the miller, and said he would wait until the wheat was ground.

"Ground!" said the proud wheat. "We are going to be ground. I hope it is agreeable. Let us keep close together."

They did keep close together, but it wasn't very agreeable to be poured into a hopper and then crushed into fine powder between two big stones.

"Makes nice flour," said the miller, rubbing it between his fingers.

"Flour!" said the wheat—which was wheat no longer. "Now I am flour, and I am finer than ever. How white I am! I really would rather be white than green or gold colour. I wonder where the learned grain is, and if it is as fine and white as I am?"

But the learned grain and her family had been laid away in the granary for seed wheat.

Before the waggon reached the house again, the two boys were fast asleep in the bottom of it, and had to be helped out just as the sack was, and carried in.

The sack was taken into the kitchen at once and opened, and even in its wheat days the flour had never been so proud as it was when it heard the farmer's wife say—

"I'm going to make this into cake."

"Ah!" it said; "I thought so. Now I shall be rich, and admired by everybody."

The farmer's wife then took some of it out in a large white bowl, and after that she busied herself beating eggs and sugar and butter all together in another bowl: and after a while she took the flour and beat it in also.

"Now I am in grand company," said the flour. "The eggs and butter are the colour of gold, the sugar is like silver or diamonds. This is the very society for me."

"The cake looks rich," said one of the daughters.

"It's rather too rich for them children," said her mother. "But Lawsey, I dunno, neither. Nothin' don't hurt 'em. I reckon they could eat a panel of rail fence and come to no harm."

"I'm rich," said the flour to itself. "That is just what I intended from the first. I am rich and I am a cake."

Just then, a pair of big brown eyes came and peeped into it. They belonged to a round little head with a mass of tangled curls all over it—they belonged to Vivian.

"What's that?" he asked.

"Cake."

"Who made it?"

"I did."

"I like you," said Vivian. "You're such a nice woman. Who's going to eat any of it? Is Lionel?"

"I'm afraid it's too rich for boys," said the woman, but she laughed and kissed him.

"No," said Vivian. "I'm afraid it isn't."

"I shall be much too rich," said the cake, angrily. "Boys, indeed. I was made for something better than boys."

After that, it was poured into a cake-mould, and put into the oven, where it had rather an unpleasant time of it. It was so hot in there that if the farmer's wife had not watched it carefully, it would have been burned.

"But I am cake," it said, "and of the richest kind, so I can bear it, even if it is uncomfortable."

When it was taken out, it really was cake, and it felt as if it was quite satisfied. Everyone who came into the kitchen and saw it, said—

"Oh, what a nice cake! How well your new flour has done!"

But just once, while it was cooling, it had a curious, disagreeable feeling. It found, all at once, that the two boys, Lionel and Vivian, had come quietly into the kitchen and stood near the table, looking at the cake with their great eyes wide open and their little red mouths open, too.

"Dear me," it said. "How nervous I feel—actually nervous. What great eyes they have, and how they shine! and what are those sharp white things in their mouths? I really don't like them to look at me in that way. It seems like something personal. I wish the farmer's wife would come."

Such a chill ran over it, that it was quite cool when the woman came in, and she put it away in the cupboard on a plate.

But, that very afternoon, she took it out again and set it on the table on a glass cake-stand. She put some leaves around it to make it look nice, and it noticed there were a great many other things on the table, and they all looked fresh and bright.

"This is all in my honour," it said. "They know I am rich."

Then several people came in and took chairs around the table.

"They all come to sit and look at me," said the vain cake. "I wish the learned grain could see me now."

There was a little high-chair on each side of the table, and at first these were empty, but in a few minutes the door opened and in came the two little boys. They had pretty, clean dresses on, and their "bangs" and curls were bright with being brushed.

"Even they have been dressed up to do me honour," thought the cake.

But, the next minute, it began to feel quite nervous again. Vivian's chair was near the glass stand, and when he had climbed up and seated himself, he put one elbow on the table and rested his fat chin on his fat hand, and fixing his eyes on the cake, sat and stared at it in such an unnaturally quiet manner for some seconds, that any cake might well have felt nervous.

"There's the cake," he said, at last, in such a deeply thoughtful voice that the cake felt faint with anger.

Then a remarkable thing happened. Some one drew the stand toward them and took the knife and cut out a large slice of the cake.

"Go away!" said the cake, though no one heard it. "I am cake! I am rich! I am not for boys! How dare you?"

Vivian stretched out his hand; he took the slice; he lifted it up, and then the cake saw his red mouth open— yes, open wider than it could have believed possible— wide enough to show two dreadful rows of little sharp white things.

"Good gra——" it began.

But it never said "cious." Never at all. For in two minutes Vivian had eaten it!!

And there was an end of its airs and graces.

Behind the White Brick

It began with Aunt Hetty's being out of temper, which, it must be confessed, was nothing new. At its best, Aunt Hetty's temper was none of the most charming, and this morning it was at its worst. She had awakened to the consciousness of having a hard day's work before her, and she had awakened late, and so everything had gone wrong from the first. There was a sharp ring in her voice when she came to Jem's bedroom door and called out, "Jemima, get up this minute!"

Jem knew what to expect when Aunt Hetty began a day by calling her "Jemima." It was one of the poor child's grievances that she had been given such an ugly name. In all the books she had read, and she had read a great many, Jem never had met a heroine who was called Jemima. But it had been her mother's favorite sister's name, and so it had fallen to her lot. Her mother always called her "Jem," or "Mimi," which was much prettier, and even Aunt Hetty only reserved Jemima for unpleasant state occasions.

It was a dreadful day to Jem. Her mother was not at home, and would not be until night. She had been called away unexpectedly, and had been obliged to leave Jem and the baby to Aunt Hetty's mercies.

So Jem found herself busy enough. Scarcely had she finished doing one thing, when Aunt Hetty told her to begin another. She wiped dishes and picked fruit and attended to the baby; and when baby had gone to sleep, and everything else seemed disposed of, for a time, at least, she was so tired that she was glad to sit down.

And then she thought of the book she had been reading the night before—a certain delightful story book, about a little girl whose name was Flora, and who was so happy and rich and pretty and good that Jem had likened her to the little princesses one reads about, to whose christening feast every fairy brings a gift.

"I shall have time to finish my chapter before dinnertime comes," said Jem, and she sat down snugly in one corner of the wide, old fashioned fireplace.

But she had not read more than two pages before something dreadful happened. Aunt Hetty came into the room in a great hurry—in such a hurry, indeed, that she caught her foot in the matting and fell, striking her elbow sharply against a chair, which so upset her temper that the moment she found herself on her feet she flew at Jem.

"What!" she said, snatching the book from her, "reading again, when I am running all over the house for you?" And she flung the pretty little blue covered volume into the fire.

Jem sprang to rescue it with a cry, but it was impossible to reach it; it had fallen into a great hollow of red coal, and the blaze caught it at once.

"You are a wicked woman!" cried Jem, in a dreadful passion, to Aunt Hetty. "You are a wicked woman."

Then matters reached a climax. Aunt Hetty boxed her ears, pushed her back on her little footstool, and walked out of the room.

Jem hid her face on her arms and cried as if her heart would break. She cried until her eyes were heavy, and she thought she would be obliged to go to sleep. But just as she was thinking of going to sleep, something fell down the chimney and made her look up. It was a piece of mortar, and it brought a good deal of soot with it. She bent forward and looked up to see where it had come from. The chimney was so very wide that this was easy enough. She could see where the mortar had fallen from the side and left a white patch.

"How white it looks against the black!" said Jem; "it is like a white brick among the black ones. What a queer place a chimney is! I can see a bit of the blue sky, I think."

And then a funny thought came into her fanciful little head. What a many things were burned in the big fireplace and vanished in smoke or tinder up the chimney! Where did everything go? There was Flora, for instance—Flora who was represented on the frontispiece—with lovely, soft, flowing hair, and a little fringe on her pretty round forehead, crowned with a circlet of daisies, and a laugh in her wide-awake round eyes. Where was she by this time? Certainly there was nothing left of her in the fire. Jem almost began to cry again at the thought.

"It was too bad," she said. "She was so pretty and funny, and I did like her so."

I daresay it scarcely will be credited by unbelieving people when I tell them what happened next, it was such a very singular thing, indeed.

Jem felt herself gradually lifted off her little footstool.

"Oh!" she said, timidly, "I fell very light." She did feel light, indeed. She felt so light that she was sure she was rising gently in the air.

"Oh," she said again, "how—how very light I feel! Oh, dear, I'm going up the chimney!"

It was rather strange that she never thought of calling for help, but she did not. She was not easily frightened; and now she was only wonderfully astonished, as she remembered afterwards. She shut her eyes tight and gave a little gasp.

"I've heard Aunt Hetty talk about the draught drawing things up the chimney, but I never knew it was as strong as this," she said.

She went up, up, up, quietly and steadily, and without any uncomfortable feeling at all; and then all at once she stopped, feeling that her feet rested against something solid. She opened her eyes and looked about her, and there she was, standing right opposite the white brick, her feet on a tiny ledge.

"Well," she said, "this is funny."

But the next thing that happened was funnier still. She found that, without thinking what she was doing, she was knocking on the white brick with her knuckles, as if it was a door and she expected somebody to open it. The next minute she heard footsteps, and then a sound, as if some one was drawing back a little bolt.

"It is a door," said Jem, "and somebody is going to open it."

The white brick moved a little, and some more mortar and soot fell; then the brick moved a little more, and then it slid aside and left an open space.

"It's a room!" cried Jem. "There's a room behind it!"

And so there was, and before the open space stood a pretty little girl, with long lovely hair and a fringe on her forehead. Jem clasped her hands in amazement. It was Flora herself, as she looked in the picture, and Flora stood laughing and nodding.

"Come in," she said. "I thought it was you."

"But how can I come in through such a little place?" asked Jem.

"Oh, that is easy enough," said Flora. "Here, give me your hand."

Jem did as she told her, and found that it was easy enough. In an instant she had passed through the opening, the white brick had gone back to its place, and she was standing by Flora's side in a large room—the nicest room she had ever seen. It was big and lofty and light, and there were all kinds of delightful things in it—books and flowers and playthings and pictures, and in one corner a great cage full of lovebirds.

"Have I ever seen it before?" asked Jem, glancing slowly around.

"Yes," said Flora; "you saw it last night—in your mind. Don't you remember it?"

Jem shook her head.

"I feel as if I did, but——"

"Why," said Flora, laughing, "it's my room, the one you read about last night."

"So it is," said Jem. "But how did you come here?"

"I can't tell you that; I myself don't know. But I am here, and so"—rather mysteriously—"are a great many other things."

"Are they?" said Jem, very much interested. "What things? Burned things? I was just wondering——"

"Not only burned things," said Flora, nodding. "Just come with me and I'll show you something."

She led the way out of the room and down a little passage with several doors in each side of it, and she opened one door and showed Jem what was on the other side of it. That was a room, too, and this time it was funny as well as pretty. Both floor and walls was strewn with toys. There were big soft balls, rattles, horses, woolly dogs, and a doll or so; there was one low cushioned chair and a low table.

"You can come in," said a shrill little voice behind the door, "only mind you don't tread on things."

"What a funny little voice!" said Jem, but she had no sooner said it than she jumped back.

The owner of the voice, who had just come forward, was no other than Baby.

"Why," exclaimed Jem, beginning to feel frightened, "I left you fast asleep in your crib."

"Did you?" said Baby, somewhat scornfully. "That's just the way with you grown-up people. You think you know everything, and yet you haven't discretion enough to know when a pin is sticking into one. You'd know soon enough if you had one sticking into your own back."

"But I'm not grown up," stammered Jem; "and when you are at home you can neither walk nor talk. You're not six months old."

"Well, miss," retorted Baby, whose wrongs seemed to have soured her disposition somewhat, "you have no need to throw that in my teeth; you were not six months old, either, when you were my age."

Jem could not help laughing.

"You haven't got any teeth," she said.

"Haven't I? said Baby, and she displayed two beautiful rows with some haughtiness of manner. "When I am up here," she said, "I am supplied with the modern conveniences, and that's why I never complain. Do I ever cry when I am asleep? It's not falling asleep I 'object to, it's falling awake."

"Wait a minute," said Jem. "Are you asleep now?"

"I'm what you call asleep. I can only come here when I'm what you call asleep. Asleep, indeed! It's no wonder we always cry when we have to fall awake."

"But we don't mean to be unkind to you," protested Jem, meekly.

She could not help thinking Baby was very severe.

"Don't mean!" said Baby. "Well, why don't you think more, then? How would you like to have all the nice things snatched away from you, and all the old rubbish packed off on you, as if you hadn't any sense? How would you like to have to sit and stare at things you wanted, and not to be able to reach them, or, if you did reach them, have them fall out of your hand, and roll away in the most unfeeling manner? And then be scolded and called 'cross!' It's no wonder we are bald. You'd be bald yourself. It's trouble and worry that keep us bald until we can begin to take care of ourselves; I had more hair than this at first, but it fell off, as well it might. No philosopher ever thought of that, I suppose!"

"Well," said Jem, in despair, "I hope you enjoy yourself when you are here?"

"Yes, I do," answered Baby. "That's one comfort. There is nothing to knock my head against, and things have patent stoppers on them, so that they can't roll away, and everything is soft and easy to pick up."

There was a slight pause after this, and Baby seemed to cool down.

"I suppose you would like me to show you round?" she said.

"Not if you have any objection," replied Jem, who was rather subdued.

"I would as soon do it as not," said Baby. "You are not as bad as some people, though you do get my clothes twisted when you hold me."

Upon the whole, she seemed rather proud of her position. It was evident she quite regarded herself as hostess. She held her small bald head very high indeed, as she trotted on before them. She stopped at the first door she came to, and knocked three times. She was obliged to stand upon tiptoe to reach the knocker.

"He's sure to be at home at this time of year," she remarked. "This is the busy season."

"Who's 'he'?" inquired Jem.

But Flora only laughed at Miss Baby's consequential air.

"S. C., to be sure," was the answer, as the young lady pointed to the door-plate, upon which Jem noticed, for the first time, "S. C." in very large letters.

The door opened, apparently without assistance, and they entered the apartment.

"Good gracious!" exclaimed Jem, the next minute. "Good*ness* gracious!"

She might well be astonished. It was such a long room that she could not see to the end of it, and it was piled up from floor to ceiling with toys of every description, and there was such bustle and buzzing in it that it was quite confusing. The bustle and buzzing arose from a very curious cause, too,—it was the bustle and buzz of hundreds of tiny men and women who were working at little tables no higher than mushrooms,—the pretty tiny women cutting out and sewing, the pretty tiny men sawing and hammering and all talking at once. The principal person in the place escaped Jem's notice at first; but it was not long before she saw him,—a little old gentleman, with a rosy face and sparkling eyes, sitting at a desk, and writing in a book almost as big as himself. He was so busy that he was quite excited, and had been obliged to throw his white fur coat and cap aside, and he was at work in his red waistcoat.

"Look here, if you please," piped Baby. "I have brought some one to see you."

When he turned round, Jem recognized him at once.

"Eh! Eh!" he said. "What! What! Who's this, Tootsicums?"

Baby's manner became very acid indeed.

"I shouldn't have thought you would have said that, Mr. Claus," she remarked. "I can't help myself down below, but I generally have my rights respected up here. I should like to know what sane godfather or godmother would give one the name of 'Tootsicums' in one's baptism. They are bad enough, I must say; but I never heard of any of them calling a person 'Tootsicums.'"

"Come, come!" said S. C., chuckling comfortably and rubbing his hands. "Don't be too dignified,—it's a bad thing. And don't be too fond of flourishing your rights in people's faces,—that's the worst of all, Miss Midget. Folks who make such a fuss about their rights turn them into wrongs sometimes."

Then he turned suddenly to Jem.

"You are the little girl from down below," he said.

"Yes, sir," answered Jem. "I'm Jem, and this is my friend Flora,—out of the blue book."

"I'm happy to make her acquaintance," said S. C., "and I'm happy to make yours. You are a nice child, though a trifle peppery. I'm very glad to see you."

"I'm very glad indeed to see you, sir," said Jem. "I wasn't quite sure——"

But there she stopped, feeling that it would be scarcely polite to tell him that she had begun of late years to lose faith in him.

But S. C. only chuckled more comfortably than ever and rubbed his hands again.

"Ho, ho!" he said. "You know who I am, then?"

Jem hesitated a moment, wondering whether it would not be taking a liberty to mention his name without putting "Mr." before it; then she remembered what Baby had called him.

"Baby called you 'Mr. Claus,' sir," she replied; "and I have seen pictures of you."

"To be sure," said S. C. "S. Claus, Esquire, of Chimneyland. How do you like me?"

"Very much," answered Jem; "very much, indeed, sir."

"Glad of it! Glad of it! But what was it you were going to say you were not quite sure of?"

Jem blushed a little.

"I was not quite sure that—that you were true, sir. At least I have not been quite sure since I have been older."

S. C. rubbed the bald part of his head and gave a little sigh.

"I hope I have not hurt your feelings, sir," faltered Jem, who was a very kind hearted little soul.

"Well, no," said S. C. "Not exactly. And it is not your fault either. It is natural, I suppose; at any rate, it is the way of the world. People lose their belief in a great many things as they grow older; but that does not make the things not true, thank goodness! and their faith often comes back after a while. But, bless me!" he added, briskly, "I'm moralizing, and who thanks a man for doing that? Suppose——"

"Black eyes or blue, sir?" said a tiny voice close to them.

Jem and Flora turned round, and saw it was one of the small workers who was asking the question.

"Whom for?" inquired S. C.

"Little girl in the red brick house at the corner," said the workwoman; "name of Birdie."

"Excuse me a moment," said S. C. to the children, and he turned to the big book and began to run his fingers down the pages in a business-like manner. "Ah! here she is!" he exclaimed at last. "Blue eyes, if you please, Thistle, and golden hair. And let it be a big one. She takes good care of them."

"Yes, sir," said Thistle; "I am personally acquainted with several dolls in her family. I go to parties in her dolls' house sometimes when she is fast asleep at night, and they all speak very highly of her. She is most attentive to them when they are ill. In fact, her pet doll is a cripple, with a stiff leg."

She ran back to her work and S. C. finished his sentence.

"Suppose I show you my establishment," he said. "Come with me."

It really would be quite impossible to describe the wonderful things he showed them. Jem's head was quite in a whirl before she had seen one-half of them, and even Baby condescended to become excited.

"There must be a great many children in the world, Mr. Claus," ventured Jem.

"Yes, yes, millions of 'em; bless 'em," said S. C., growing rosier with delight at the very thought. "We never run out of them, that's one comfort. There's a large and varied assortment always on hand. Fresh ones every year, too, so that when one grows too old there is a new one ready. I have a place like this in every twelfth chimney. Now it's boys, now it's girls, always one or t'other; and there's no end of playthings for them, too, I'm glad to say. For girls, the great thing seems to be dolls. Blitzen! what comfort they *do* take in dolls! but the boys are for horses and racket."

They were standing near a table where a worker was just putting the finishing touch to the dress of a large wax doll, and just at that moment, to Jem's surprise, she set it on the floor, upon its feet, quite coolly.

"Thank you," said the doll, politely.

Jem quite jumped.

"You can join the rest now and introduce yourself," said the worker.

The doll looked over her shoulder at her train.

"It hangs very nicely," she said. "I hope it's the latest fashion."

"Mine never talked like that," said Flora. "My best one could only say 'Mamma,' and it said it very badly, too."

"She was foolish for saying it at all," remarked the doll, haughtily. "We don't talk and walk before ordinary people;

we keep our accomplishments for our own amusement, and for the amusement of our friends. If you should chance to get up in the middle of the night, some time, or should run into the room suddenly some day, after you have left it, you might hear—but what is the use of talking to human beings?"

"You know a great deal, considering you are only just finished," snapped Baby, who really was a Tartar.

"I was FINISHED," retorted the doll. "I did not begin life as a baby!" very scornfully.

"Pooh!" said Baby. "We improve as we get older."

"I hope so, indeed," answered the doll. "There is plenty of room for improvement." And she walked away in great state.

S. C. looked at Baby and then shook his head. "I shall not have to take very much care of you," he said, absent-mindedly. "You are able to take pretty good care of yourself."

"I hope I am," said Baby, tossing her head.

S. C. gave his head another shake.

"Don't take too good care of yourself," he said. "That's a bad thing, too."

He showed them the rest of his wonders, and then went with them to the door to bid them good-bye.

"I am sure we are very much obliged to you, Mr. Claus," said Jem, gratefully. "I shall never again think you are not true, sir."

S. C. patted her shoulder quite affectionately.

"That's right," he said. "Believe in things just as long as you can, my dear. Good-bye until Christmas Eve. I shall see you then, if you don't see me."

He must have taken quite a fancy to Jem, for he stood looking at her, and seemed very reluctant to close the door, and even after he had closed it, and they had turned away, he opened it a little again to call to her.

"Believe in things as long as you can, my dear."

"How kind he is!" exclaimed Jem, full of pleasure.

Baby shrugged her shoulders.

"Well enough in his way," she said, "but rather inclined to prose and be old-fashioned."

Jem looked at her, feeling rather frightened, but she said nothing.

Baby showed very little interest in the next room she took them to.

"I don't care about this place," she said, as she threw open the door. "It has nothing but old things in it. It is the Nobody-knows-where room."

She had scarcely finished speaking before Jem made a little spring and picked something up.

"Here's my old strawberry pincushion!" she cried out. And then, with another jump and another dash at two or three other things, "And here's my old fairy-book! And here's my little locket I lost last summer! How did they come here?"

"They went Nobody-knows-where," said Baby. "And this is it."

"But cannot I have them again?" asked Jem.

"No," answered Baby. "Things that go to Nobody-knows-where stay there."

"Oh!" sighed Jem, "I am so sorry."

"They are only old things," said Baby.

"But I like my old things," said Jem. "I love them. And there is mother's needle case. I wish I might take that. Her dead little sister gave it to her, and she was so sorry when she lost it."

"People ought to take better care of their things," remarked Baby.

Jem would have liked to stay in this room and wander about among her old favorites for a long time, but Baby was in a hurry.

"You'd better come away," she said. "Suppose I was to have to fall awake and leave you?"

The next place they went into was the most wonderful of all.

"This is the Wish room," said Baby. "Your wishes come

here—yours and mother's, and Aunt Hetty's and father's and mine. When did you wish that?"

Each article was placed under a glass shade, and labelled with the words and name of the wishers. Some of them were beautiful, indeed; but the tall shade Baby nodded at when she asked her question was truly alarming, and caused Jem a dreadful pang of remorse. Underneath it sat Aunt Hetty, with her mouth stitched up so that she could not speak a word, and beneath the stand was a label bearing these words, in large black letters—

"I wish Aunt Hetty's mouth was sewed up, Jem."

"Oh, dear!" cried Jem, in great distress. "How it must have hurt her! How unkind of me to say it! I wish I hadn't wished it. I wish it would come undone."

She had no sooner said it than her wish was gratified. The old label disappeared and a new one showed itself, and there sat Aunt Hetty, looking herself again, and even smiling.

Jem was grateful beyond measure, but Baby seemed to consider her weak minded.

"It served her right," she said.

But when, after looking at the wishes at the end of the room, they went to the other end, her turn came. In one corner stood a shade with a baby under it, and the baby was Miss Baby herself, but looking as she very rarely looked; in fact, it was the brightest, best tempered baby one could imagine.

"I wish I had a better tempered baby. Mother," was written on the label.

Baby became quite red in the face with anger and confusion.

"That wasn't here the last time I came," she said. "And it is right down mean in mother!"

This was more than Jem could bear.

"It wasn't mean," she said. "She couldn't help it. You know you are a cross baby—everybody says so."

Baby turned two shades redder.

"Mind your own business," she retorted. "It was mean; and as to that silly little thing being better than I am," turning up her small nose, which was quite turned up enough by Nature—"I must say I don't see anything so very grand about her. So, there!"

She scarcely condescended to speak to them while they remained in the Wish room, and when they left it, and went to the last door in the passage, she quite scowled at it.

"I don't know whether I shall open it at all," she said.

"Why not?" asked Flora. "You might as well."

"It is the Lost pin room," she said. "I hate pins."

She threw the door open with a bang, and then stood and shook her little fist viciously. The room was full of pins, stacked solidly together. There were hundreds of them—thousands—millions, it seemed.

"I'm glad they *are* lost!" she said. "I wish there were more of them there."

"I didn't know there were so many pins in the world," said Jem.

"Pooh!" said Baby. "Those are only the lost ones that have belonged to our family."

After this they went back to Flora's room and sat down, while Flora told Jem the rest of her story.

"Oh!" sighed Jem, when she came to the end. "How delightful it is to be here! Can I never come again?"

"In one way you can," said Flora. "When you want to come, just sit down and be as quiet as possible, and shut your eyes and think very hard about it. You can see everything you have seen to-day, if you try."

"Then I shall be sure to try," Jem answered. She was going to ask some other question, but Baby stopped her.

"Oh! I'm falling awake," she whimpered, crossly, rubbing her eyes. "I'm falling awake again."

And then, suddenly, a very strange feeling came over Jem. Flora and the pretty room seemed to fade away, and, without being able to account for it at all, she found herself sitting on her little stool again, with a beautiful

scarlet and gold book on her knee, and her mother standing by laughing at her amazed face. As to Miss Baby, she
was crying as hard as she could in her crib.

"Mother!" Jem cried out, "have you really come home
so early as this, and—and," rubbing her eyes in great
amazement, "how did I come down?"

"Don't I look as if I was real?" said her mother, laughing
and kissing her. "And doesn't your present look real? I
don't know how you came down, I'm sure. Where have
you been?"

Jem shook her head very mysteriously. She saw that
her mother fancied she had been asleep, but she herself
knew better.

"I know you wouldn't believe it was true if I told you,"
she said; "I have been

BEHIND THE WHITE BRICK."